Elegance & Simplicity

Elegance & Simplicity

a novel

Ronald G. Munro

Published by Tate Publishing & Enterprises, LLC
127 E. Trade Center Terrace | Mustang, Oklahoma 73064 USA
1.888.361.9473 | www.tatepublishing.com

Tate Publishing is committed to excellence in the publishing industry. The company reflects the philosophy established by the founders, based on Psalm 68:11,
"The Lord gave the word and great was the company of those who published it."

Cover design by Christina Hicks
Interior design by Joel Uber

Published in the United States of America

ISBN: 978-1-61346-736-7
1. Fiction: Romance, Historical
2. Fiction: Historical
11.10.10

Dedication

For Carolyn, whose understated elegance instills genuine appreciation for even the simplest matters in life.

Acknowledgments

The author wishes to express his unending gratitude to his wife, Carolyn, and to our dear friend, Virginia Lee, both avid Jane Austenites, and to Jack Lee, an accomplished eighteenth-century dancer, for their critical reading of the manuscript and for their unswerving encouragement. Thanks also are due to our dear friend, Barbara Ziman, who has been, for many years, an invaluable guide in all matters pertaining to the proper accouterments of the Regency and Federal periods. Additionally, sincere appreciation is rendered to the Jane Austen Centre in Bath, England, for its annual presentation of the Jane Austen Festival; participation in that wonderful festival stimulated the author's imagination to conceive and write this story.

Chapter 1

Virtue has much in common with folly when it is clothed in dissimulation rather than arrayed in the radiance of simplicity. Mankind too often has forgotten this truth. Fortunately, womankind has had the perspicacity to remind them of it, often.

Miss Ariana Atwood was one such young woman, possessed of the confidence expected of someone inclined to a practical persuasion and endowed with an expressive demeanor, which, if not charming, was usually of an agreeable nature. Suitors privileged to experience her thoroughly concise and thoughtful opinions rarely contradicted her, and few gave cause for the occasion to be repeated.

"I do not believe that I shall ever marry," remarked Miss Ariana, "for I have neither the temperament for expedience nor the facility for idleness."

Mrs. Atwood displayed the most censuring frown that could be afforded a proper lady who was being indecorously jostled in an unruly carriage, each pitch and roll of the carriage delineating the character of the country road recently washed to roughness by an early spring rain, which, as was widely declared, had pretensions of being a deluge.

"Do not think you can vex me with such nonsense," she declared to her eldest daughter. "Today, my humor is unimpeachable. I am overjoyed that we can at last undertake our annual journey to Bath, and I shall brook no nonsense. No, indeed, I shall not take notice of it, no matter what address you shall give it."

"Then let that be the end of it," replied Ariana amiably, "for I am too much inclined today to appreciate the fairness of these fields and meadows than to be diverted by the excesses of melancholy philosophy."

"Quite," said Mr. Atwood, who otherwise sat quietly in blissful inattention to his wife and two daughters.

Suddenly distracted, Miss Gwyneth declared with some astonishment, "Look there! There!" she emphasized with sufficient urgency as to startle everyone. "Is that not a carriage approaching Southjoy Mission?"

"It is most certainly a carriage," said Ariana, looking where Gwyneth pointed, "but as to whether or not it is stopping at Southjoy Mission, I cannot say."

"It most certainly is not stopping," declared Mrs. Atwood, with only a little umbrage toward Ariana's obstinacy. "No one of any reputation would consider stopping at Southjoy Mission."

"I suppose," said Gwyneth, unconvinced. "Perhaps it is merely a traveler who has heard of its Spanish arches," she offered. "I have heard that people from quite far away come to admire them, and I should not be surprised if they wanted a closer view of them."

Ariana smiled pleasantly at her sister. It was not its reputation for arches that would intrigue the interest of most people regarding Southjoy Mission. Gwyneth, however, had that most rare facility of perceiving in the constitution of any person or situation some redeeming quality, however remote, and allowing for it with a natural and sincere acceptance. Turning again to look in the direction of Southjoy Mission, Ariana remarked somewhat absently, "I have always thought it a forlorn beauty, abandoned early in its youth yet remaining graceful despite its years of neglect."

As the distant carriage disappeared from view behind the rise of a small knoll, Ariana ventured to tease, "Perhaps it was not a carriage at all. Perhaps it was only the ghostly return of the Infamous Merchant come to reclaim his property."

"Ariana! Do not speak with such impertinence," scoffed Mrs. Atwood. "Of course there was a carriage. I saw it with my own eyes, and so did you, and it did not stop, and if it did stop, you can be sure it was at the direction of a gentleman of considerable means."

"But surely not Mr. Stacey, the inheritor," remarked Ariana factually. "It is widely spoken that Mr. Stacey has no taste for country living and much prefers the more ardent pace set in London."

"I have heard it so," agreed Mrs. Atwood, "and he is seldom seen elsewhere. So," she added, ever faithful to her premise, "if there is an interest in Southjoy Mission, it must come from some other gentleman."

"A gentleman," repeated Gwyneth. "I should like that, but a gentleman without a wife, someone who would be free to win the admiration of Southjoy Mission."

"A gentleman," continued Ariana, "who would perceive its noble dignity."

"A gentleman," declared Mrs. Atwood firmly, "who would require a wife to lend a woman's touch to soften the demeanor of Southjoy Mission."

To those truths universally acknowledged must be appended this: that an unattended manor of substantial fortune and circumstance must be in want of a lady's attention. No truer example may be supposed than that afforded by Southjoy Mission, whose former disposition was colored by its reputedly sanguine history related to the persecution of heretics in England, most especially the Lollards. Its original construction began in 1490 when a wealthy member of the Spanish nobility commissioned the building of a small palatial retreat in anticipation of a royal wedding between the courts of Spain and England which would have secured peace between those two realms. When the propitious marriage was significantly delayed, the disgruntled nobleman offered it for use as a monastery. For a number of years, it was a secluded place heavily ensconced with mystery, and it was said that Lollards were detained and tortured there, though it was never proven so. The suspicion, though, was sufficient to incline the local population to a wariness that quickly emigrated to an unmitigated rumor of a curse. That conviction was emboldened by a century of intemperate use which left the mansion in the sufferance of neglect and disrepair. The mansion was reclaimed briefly by a wealthy merchant, but he himself suffered a series of scandalous interludes that cast him into disrepute and rendered him derelict of fortune.

Thereafter, Southjoy Mission fell into progressive desolation, being revived and abandoned at various times for nearly seven decades, until it was purchased by the renowned and much admired Sir Waverly Sylvia who desired to acquire the land appertaining to the Mission and being nearly adjacent to his own holdings. Southjoy Mission conveyed to Sir Waverly as part of the transaction. Though sternly warned of the Mission's sanguinary history, Sir Waverly found the Mission to be admirably situated and capable of serving as the manor house of a great estate. With his much noted verve, Sir Waverly undertook to renovate the property in its entirety. In tribute to his wife, Lady Sylvia, who much admired its Spanish arches, Sir Waverly chose to preserve the outward appearance of the Mission while adding to its internal constitution only those conveniences essential to modern living.

Alas, the renovation had but scarcely commenced when Sir Waverly met with a sudden and unaccountable demise, confirming, in the minds of many, the persistence of a dark and unrelenting curse on Southjoy Mission.

As required by the legal prescription of his will, Sir Waverly's properties and considerable fortune were entailed to his eldest nephew, Mr. Cedric Stacey. The latter gentleman, for surely he was presumed to be a gentleman, was little known outside of London, whose society he was said to prefer. Indeed, no one in the vicinity of Southjoy Mission could ascribe to any acquaintance with Mr. Stacey, nor could anyone account for his apparent disdain for his newly acquired neighbors. In consequence, neither Mr. Stacey nor any other occupant was to be observed at Southjoy Mission for above a year, and both lord and manor faded from common discussion until a carriage was reportedly observed stopping at Southjoy Mission.

The expedition to Bath was, by all accounts and from all parties, a decidedly satisfying excursion. Mrs. Atwood, Ariana, and Gwyneth were most ardent in their perusal of the shops on Pulteney Bridge and their exploration of every fashionable shop within walking distance thereof. Mrs. Atwood was enthralled with the purchase of a new bonnet of modest design, which also had the virtue of being not extravagant in cost.

Gwyneth, who had quietly anticipated the opportunity to purchase a length of fabric suitable for a gown, was most excited by the silk fabrics displayed in the shops near the spa, though she eventually settled for a quite worthy selection of white muslin.

For her part, Ariana stood in the lace shop looking very longingly at an eloquent sarcenet spencer, articulated with hand embroidery and a very fine trim of Bucks Point Lace but had to content herself with admiration only in respect of its price. Even such admiration, however, was not without a cost of its own, for as Ariana ever so delicately examined the detail in the lace, she herself was the object of a much less delicate scrutiny.

"Still with pretensions that exceed your station, I see," observed Mrs. Crandesol in her redoubtably caustic tone. "It will do you no good, no good whatsoever. You have not the breeding to it."

In her surprise, Ariana scarcely had time to turn and reply, "Mrs. Crandesol, a good day to you, and how kind of you to remember me."

Mrs. Crandesol, however, had already turned away, not having further attention to spare for the likes of Miss Ariana Atwood.

"A most unpleasant woman," remarked Mrs. Atwood gruffly, as she quickly joined Ariana, though she sensibly elected not to pursue the full expression of her displeasure until she could do so without fear of retribution and in the company of Mr. Atwood.

Fortunately, a minor pit in the facade of a great monument does not mar its luster, nor could one such unpleasantry begin to mar the multitude of memorable occasions afforded to a visitor in Bath. A simple promenade along the River Avon was more than enough to banish that scene from memory, especially when Mr. Carlton Garrick might be found sketching Pulteney Bridge from one of its shores. Mr. Garrick was a particular friend of Gwyneth, but his amiable character made him well liked by all the Atwoods.

In his youth, Carlton had lived a rather common existence in London. He received a moderate education, but having developed a passion for painting and drawing, his formal education went no further. Unhappily, Carlton regarded London as rather inhospitable, for he had neither family nor fortune to recommend him, and of prospects, there were none. As a result, early one morning, he collected his belongings, which consisted of pigments, pencils, and paper, and ventured forth to discover the charm and simplicity of country towns and villages. His journey, in due course, took him to Bath where, in truth, he had not intended to stay long. Indeed, he came as a matter of curiosity to see the city that had become the rage of traveling tourists. He had expected it to be crass and thinly crusted with an ornamental appeal to the pithy and vulgar. Instead, he found splendor. He found an ancient city that was alive with youthful zeal. In short, he found a sense of belonging. It must be said, though, that Fate may have influenced that sentiment, for he was in exactly the right place at the right time to acquire a small commission to sketch a house newly built in Bathwick. The commission was sufficiently small as to seem insignificant to others of his trade, but for Carlton, it was the first sign of a future. It also introduced him to Mr. Andrew Cunnings, whose father had served as the coordinator and facilitator for the construction of the house. Andrew, who was a very unassuming young man himself, soon came to regard Carlton as a talented and amiable artist. Andrew extended a sympathetic friendship to Carlton, which quickly gravitated to genuine friendship, and it was through Andrew that Carlton began to make acquaintances in Bath, one of whom was Miss Gwyneth Atwood. Gwyneth and Carlton, it seems, shared an instant empathy. They had a mutually sensitive and unpretentious regard for the simplest of truths in the most ordinary and unexceptional occurrences. Neither seemed to regard the inauspicious fortune of the other as a detriment, which is good and proper in the course of love, for the only measure of wealth acknowledged by love is reciprocity.

The Atwoods, as a whole, pursued their opportunities to renew old friendships and acquaintances with much zeal, but, in truth, it was their visit to the Pump Room and the ritual of taking the waters at the spa that made the journey to Bath complete. Indeed, that occasion so refreshed the ladies that they would later remark that, had they no other experience in Bath but that one alone, it would have been sufficient to endear them to Bath above all other places. In consequence and by journey's end, the ladies could rightly claim, as they would be certain to inform Mr. Atwood, they had accounted for themselves as handsomely as sensible economy would permit.

Meanwhile, Mr. Atwood pursued his customary business associations through which he acquired, as it happened, news of the greatest merit and consequence to Mrs. Atwood.

On this, their last day in Bath, Mrs. Atwood, having finally set aside her new bonnet, was now concentrating on organizing in her mind the gossip she would most relish upon her return home. It seemed to her most annoying that Mr. Atwood, who cared not a wit about gossip, should have the best of it.

"Are we to understand," asked Mrs. Atwood with not a little agitation, "that Southjoy Mission is finally to be occupied?"

Mr. Atwood nodded indifferently. "It seems it is so, my dear. I have it on the reliable authority of Mr. Cunnings, who has been retained to see the manor prepared for the new occupant's arrival. I say 'new occupant' and not 'Mr. Stacey' for I have been told, as you have predicted, my dear, the occupant is not to be the elusive Mr. Stacey at all."

"If not Mr. Stacey, then it is to be let?" inquired Ariana.

"Impossible," scoffed Mrs. Atwood. "I cannot believe there is anyone who does not see Southjoy Mission as a vindictive, cursed monster."

"I am sorry to hear it," remarked Mr. Atwood, pausing to look up from the book he was absently perusing, "for I understand that it is to be occupied by Sir Waverly's widow, Lady Sylvia, with whom, I recall, you are somewhat acquainted."

"What?" cried Mrs. Atwood. "Lady Sylvia! Oh, dear me, yes! I have twice had the honor to be presented to Her Ladyship, once in London and once in Bath when she, with gracious and much admired condescension, attended a most glorious charity ball at the Upper Assembly Rooms."

"Indeed, so I have heard on numerous occasions," acknowledged Mr. Atwood. "I have it on further good authority that Mr. Stacey prefers London to the country and has invited his aunt, Lady Sylvia, to fulfill Sir Waverly's design for Southjoy Mission. It is said that Lady Sylvia is much devoted to the memory of Sir Waverly, and, a proper year of mourning having elapsed, Lady Sylvia intends to see the Mission to its rightful place in our society, as indeed her late husband envisioned it."

"Then, perhaps, there is also some measure of propriety to be acknowledged in Mr. Stacey's conduct and in his generous allowance to Lady Sylvia," remarked Miss Gwyneth. "Surely this allowance exceeds any obligation his inheritance might reasonably require of him?"

An expressive smile drew gently across Mr. Atwood's face. "The kindness of your spirit is ever a comfort," he said softly. "If we do not think well of one who has done a good deed, though we know him not, what shall we think of one we do know, who, though known to us, has not a good deed to account for his character?"

"Mr. Stacey is a gentleman by wealth," observed Ariana. "More than that we cannot venture with any certainty."

Mrs. Atwood seemed displeased that the conversation had diverted in this manner. "It is Lady Sylvia who shall occupy Southjoy Mission," she declared with an emphasis that precluded any suggestion of a contrary view.

"Indeed, you are correct, my dear. Mr. Cunnings also informs me that a somewhat distant cousin or niece of Lady Sylvia, one Isabella de la Vega, lately arrived from Spain, will accompany her. It seems that Miss Isabella, who is said to be quite young, has suffered a tragic loss of her own near relations, and Lady Sylvia has taken charge of her."

Exuding a certain degree of exaltation, Mrs. Atwood asserted, "Then she shall have great need of friendly acquaintances. Mr. Atwood! Make haste! We must be earnest in our acquaintance with Lady Sylvia, or we shall be the most socially wanting people of our society."

Chapter 2

The romance of Sir Waverly and Lady Sylvia was held in nearly legendary admiration, more perhaps by those of common birth than by those of a royal lineage. Nonetheless, propelled by this high regard, the conveyance of Southjoy Mission to Sir Waverly was thought by many to be a good omen. He was, after all, a man of many talents and great energy. He often seemed tireless in undertaking countless pursuits which inevitably enhanced his reputation and fortune. He required only that an undertaking be of worthy end in its accomplishment and of worthy challenge in its attainment. His acclaim was raised to further heights by his knighthood which, however, was bestowed only partly for the distinction and economy he achieved for the realm. More frequently noted and praised was his meritorious service in the Battle of Jersey in 1781, which in the hands of providence would prove to be of singular importance to his personal happiness. Modestly, he asserted that he had done no more in that battle than any other soldier of the realm, and indeed, he was celebrated more for what occurred after the battle than during it. Sir Waverly, who was Captain Sylvia at that time, had observed that the attack on Jersey, while bold, was not well executed. Puzzled by this, for French soldiers were renowned in their own right, Sir Waverly thought to question several of the prisoners about their reconnaissance whereupon he discovered that certain information regarding fortifications and the state of readiness had been sold to a privateer who passed it on to the French, including the suggestion that Twelfth Night festivities might distract the British defenders from their usual vigilance. The individual, one Simon Trayyar, was soon discovered and brought before a military tribunal. His defense was sufficiently aggressive as to forestall his execution for treason. Nonetheless, ample culpability of wrongdoing was established without any arguable doubt, which resulted in the man being sent to a penal colony where, as it happened, he died a short while later in a fight with another prisoner.

Unfortunately, as is often the case in matters of disgrace, it was not only the villain who suffered the penalty. The man had several children who suddenly were taken from a state of relative privilege to a state of poverty. Because their mother was deceased, it was determined that humane consideration for the children would best be served by placing them with various charitable families, whereby they might be spared a lifetime of shame. Moved to compassion himself, Sir Waverly anonymously established a small fund by which the children might not be wanting in at least a modest education. It was through this act of charity that he met Beatrice, who one day would become his wife, Lady Sylvia. When, some while later, Sir Waverly spoke of his knighthood, he never failed to comment on how strange the course of events had been, that an honor bestowed on one person was owing to the dishonor perpetrated by another.

It may have been this reputation for honor that caused many people to rejoice at Sir Waverly's acquisition of Southjoy Mission. However, whatever was hoped for in that momentous transaction was not to materialize, for Sir Waverly was not often in fair agreement with ordinary thinking, as indeed others had discovered repeatedly. Even women of substantial station, who naturally pined for his attention, were soon disabused of their fantasies. Sir Waverly was too preoccupied to respond to the frivolous pursuits most demanded of him. It was said, not unkindly, that only a woman with an iron will would satisfy Waverly Sylvia. He found such a woman in Beatrice, whom he pursued with more passion than ever he had expended on any of his praiseworthy endeavors. He found her to be as indefatigable in her works of charity as he himself was in his own pursuits, and as dedicated. It was, in essence, a common bond of spirits. Indeed, whenever he was asked if, in Beatrice, he had found his equal, he was fond of answering, "No, not an equal, for in the veritable light of truth, she has no equal."

On this point, there was wide and common agreement. Beatrice carried herself with such intrinsic dignity and noble bearing that, although she was not descended from a noble line, no one ever thought to address her by any appellation other than Lady Sylvia, as appropriate to a knight's wife, or, by reference, Her Ladyship, as appropriate to the veneration of her many public champions. In matters large and small, such was the equity of their mutual respect, it was said that Beatrice and Waverly advanced together in elegant turns and steps, one balanced against the other, like dancers performing intricate pirouettes.

So it was, too, in the matter of Southjoy Mission, for in the relocation of Her Ladyship to Southjoy Mission, there was in that movement the essence of a minuet wherein the steps of Lady Sylvia were graciously reflected and balanced by the memory of Sir Waverly.

Scarcely had a score of days transpired since the Atwoods' excursion to Bath when a letter arrived addressed to Mr. and Mrs. Atwood and bearing news of the greatest import to Mrs. Atwood.

"My dear Mr. Atwood! You cannot imagine!" declared Mrs. Atwood, intruding unannounced into Mr. Atwood's private study in a state of unbridled commotion.

"I am certain I cannot," observed Mr. Atwood, whose eyebrows were elevated in wonder at the unceremonious breach of his privacy.

"There is to be a ball at the Upper Assembly Rooms in Bath in two weeks' time to honor the arrival of Lady Sylvia, and," announced Mrs. Atwood with a certain flourish of triumph, "we are invited!"

"A fortnight," repeated Mr. Atwood, as he considered the implications of the timing. "Then we must hope the unpredictable spring rains will have abated by then, or the roads might well be impassable."

"Indeed, they shall be passable," declared Mrs. Atwood in her most imperious manner. "All shall be as right as, well," she hesitated but slightly, "as right as may be," against which clearly no envoy of contradiction would be received. "It is the best of times for a ball," insisted Mrs. Atwood, "and now, my dear," she hastened on, "you must secure lodgings for us immediately, or all the best accommodations will be let!"

"I would be much surprised if we should find, on such short notice, lodgings so admirably situated as the Royal Crescent," said Mr. Atwood thoughtfully. "However, with good fortune, we might have rooms at Sydney Hotel, just at the end of Great Pulteney Street."

"The Sydney Hotel! How absolutely perfect!" declared Mrs. Atwood. "And from there, we shall be able to hire a special carriage, perhaps even a barouche, to transport us to the ball, and a very fine carriage it shall be! Every eye will turn to us!"

"That should indeed afford a considerable advantage to any pretty girls who might happen to be in such a carriage," acknowledged Mr. Atwood. Seeing Mrs. Atwood's eyes set to a fine glimmer by the thought of it, he added, "that is, should there be an eligible gentleman there to take notice."

"Gwyneth!" cried Mrs. Atwood with sudden urgency. "Ariana!"

Sharply turning then in a flurry of agitated waving and scurrying, Mrs. Atwood departed the study in unmitigated haste, leaving Mr. Atwood suspended in a vacuum of conversation.

Lodgings at Sydney Hotel, though much in demand, were procured without serious difficulty. Dresses and adorning accouterments, such as could be secured in the brief time allotted for preparations, were packed for the journey with the utmost of attention. Even the carriage was polished with sufficient care as to be acknowledged approvingly by the esteemed residents of Bath city, for the latter, themselves, would be likewise suitably prepared for the occasion. Upon the appointed day, then, after a satisfactory entrance into the city, the Atwoods were comfortably installed in accommodations most favorable to their needs.

"I think I shall take a turn in the garden before tea," said Ariana. "We are quite settled now in our rooms, and I dare say we must relish this opportunity to see

Sydney Gardens without fail. They are, I believe, the most admired in Bath and perhaps all of England."

"Yes, indeed," responded Gwyneth, brimming with enthusiasm. "Do you think we might stroll through the whole of the labyrinth? Would it not be thrilling to know what celebrated and notable people have stepped upon these same paths?"

"I should think it would be a great delight," replied Ariana in the good humor of Gwyneth's effervescent spirit, and before any objection could be made to this proposal, they hastened to descend the staircase in search of the famous garden, which they found with no great difficulty. Their pursuit, however, was halted at the entrance to the garden, located at the rear of the hotel, by their admiration of a great transparency of Apollo, seen there as the god of music.

"Oh, Ari," breathed Gwyneth, "how absolutely magical. The lighting from behind gives the figure a nearly spiritual quality."

"To very good effect," said Ariana. "As the god of music, he was believed to be a much accomplished player of the lyre, such as you see there in the picture."

"As well any deity should be," said a deep, masculine voice behind them.

The Miss Atwoods turned about as one to confront a tall gentleman, finely dressed in a fashionable tailcoat, a handsome brocade waistcoat, and light britches set off by an elegant pair of riding boots. Ariana looked boldly at him, as there was a certain affronting air and mockery to his remark, further reinforced by a critical frown upon his face.

"You are a scholar of deities then?" asked Ariana with a boldness of her own, given that she was uncertain of the true intent of the gentleman's remark.

"Neither a scholar of deities nor a student of art," replied the gentleman, "but it requires neither to see that this display obstructs the view of the gardens, and for myself, I find that nature is a more superior artist than any mortal has expectation to be."

"I do not believe it is meant to be a competition," said Ariana, responding to the gentleman's unpleasant tone. "Art is interpretive. It is often an abstraction from nature, true, but it also bears an infusion of elements depicting human relations, not merely their physical presence."

"And yet, with scarcely a thought to the contrary, you shall walk past this caricature and into a garden that shall afford you pleasures of the mind and eye such as no work of art ever shall invent." And with an air of dismissal matching his address, he turned and was away without further word.

"Dear me," spoke Gwyneth, somewhat hushed, "I fear we have offended that gentleman, though in what manner, I cannot say."

In a tone that assured the firmness of her position, Ariana replied, "Dear Gwyny, we have nothing upon which to reproach ourselves. Such arrogance and conceit were wholly unworthy to the situation, and if there was offense, it was surely completely on his part alone."

Then, with a slight turn of her head and a graceful gesture toward the garden entrance, she added with a bemused smile, "And, now, as neither scholars of deities nor students of art, let us hasten to our walk!"

The night of the ball arrived with all the attendant excitement suited to an event at the Upper Assembly Rooms and the honored presence of her ladyship, Lady Beatrice Sylvia.

"Is she not beautiful, Father?" asked Ariana.

A slight coloring rose in the cheek of Gwyneth as Mr. Atwood turned to admire the graceful, high-waisted dress of soft muslin, capped at the shoulders with puff sleeves, that lay comfortably and to good advantage upon her figure.

"Indeed, she is," replied Mr. Atwood, "as are you both," he added, giving equal admiration to Ariana's sensibly striking white muslin frock, which, while sensible, was elevated in stylishness by the accent of a silk sash and the embroidery of fragile gauze that achieved a pleasingly delicate appearance. "I think you both must be very careful not to be too charming this evening, or you shall have every eligible gentleman paying particular attention to none other than yourselves, leaving all other young ladies in want of a partner."

Five spectacular Georgian chandeliers reached across the length of the ballroom designed by John Wood the Younger in 1769, brightly illuminating the pastel blue walls and the polished wood dance floor where now the whole of Bath's most important society congregated to pay homage to the shire's most renowned resident, Lady Sylvia. In due course and at the proper moment, Mrs. Atwood approached Her Ladyship's presence, entraining with her, at the proper distance, Ariana and Gwyneth. As they approached, a lady's attendant whispered anonymously in Lady Sylvia's ear, to which communication Her Ladyship exhibited no outward acknowledgment.

"Mrs. Atwood, a pleasure to see you once again." Turning to indicate the young lady to her side and slightly behind her, Lady Sylvia continued, "Allow me to present my niece, Miss Isabella de la Vega, who now resides with me at Southjoy Mission. My nephew, Mr. Cedric Stacey, was to attend with us this evening, but unfortunately he was called away on business only this morning."

Isabella's eyes, shimmering with a certain mixture of excitement and uncertainty, glanced particularly at Ariana as she curtsied to Mrs. Atwood and her daughters. For a young lady uprooted, displaced, and at the mercy of foreigners, she exhibited more poise than might be expected from her fifteen years of age, and if there appeared to be a hint of shyness in her manner, it could readily be excused.

Beaming with more than apparent delight, Mrs. Atwood gushed, "Oh, my dear Lady Sylvia, the pleasure and the honor are all mine. That you should remember the encounter that I cherish so dearly in my memory is more than I could ever dare to wish. And here, Lady Sylvia," she continued in delirious haste, "here are my daughters, Ariana and Gwyneth."

"I see," said Lady Sylvia toward Gwyneth, "you are the pretty one, and you," she said, turning toward Ariana, "must then be the clever one."

"Oh, indeed, Lady Sylvia, indeed," rushed Mrs. Atwood to agree. "There are no two sisters who can claim to be prettier or cleverer as a pair than my own dear daughters."

Ariana, who disliked false praise as much as censure, felt compelled to clarify her mother's appraisal, firmly but not reproachfully. "I can readily attest to Gwyneth's beauty, but as to my own cleverness, I have seen too little of the world to measure it."

Lady Sylvia canted her head ever so slightly to stare unequivocally at Ariana for fully three seconds before speaking, while Mrs. Atwood stood paling and speechless.

"Then, let us agree," said Lady Sylvia without umbrage, "that you have a spirit of some respectable boldness."

Hastening to recover from her daughter's impertinence, Mrs. Atwood declared with an exaggerated degree of shooing agitation to her tone, "Yes. Yes, that is it precisely, and how very generous of you to make such an understanding observation."

"Miss Ariana," said Lady Sylvia, ignoring Mrs. Atwood, "I am myself fond of unpretentious conversation. I would speak with you further, if you would do me the kindness of taking tea with me? I have made sufficient acquaintances for the moment, and I do recall that the tearoom here is as splendid as any to be found in London."

Ariana turned with speechless surprise to look at her mother for guidance, but Mrs. Atwood stood suddenly immobilized with one hand pressed to her mouth and the other to her heart. Seeing no assistance from that quarter, Ariana quickly rallied her own composure and, being sensible to the respect due Lady Sylvia, accepted the invitation with adequate decorum. Upon so doing, Her Ladyship turned from her present guests and led a majestic retreat into the appropriately majestic tearoom, leaving Isabella in the care of Mrs. Atwood and Gwyneth.

"Dear me, dear me," spoke Mrs. Atwood barely above a whisper, as she stared after the retreating images of Lady Sylvia and Ariana.

"Indeed," agreed Gwyneth with some degree of bemused apprehension.

"I must speak to Mr. Atwood at once," exclaimed Mrs. Atwood who departed on the instant, leaving Gwyneth, even more bemused than before, to address herself to Isabella, who smiled delightfully back at Gwyneth.

In the suddenness of the moment, Gwyneth and Isabella were simultaneously stricken with the laughter of startled relief.

With, then, the warmth of sudden friendship, Gwyneth asked, "Miss Isabella, shall we take a turn about the room to discover what adventures may lie there in store for us?"

The ballroom was crowded with diverse people arrayed in elegant attire, all speaking earnestly, exchanging pleasantries or hinted gossip, some boisterous with festivity, while others exhibited their preference to be agreeably sedate. Young gentlemen in want of a dancing partner could be found in such sufficient abundance that two young ladies passing nearby attracted many glances and a few charming smiles. But of invitations to dance, there were none.

"Ah, there," said Gwyneth with a warming smile, as she directed Isabella's attention to a small group standing together in a semblance of respectable demeanor. "There is Mr. Cunnings and his party."

Taking Isabella by the hand, Gwyneth skillfully navigated the remaining crowd to arrive before a delighted Mr. Cunnings, who bowed deeply in recognition of the honor accorded him.

"You know, of course, Mr. Cunnings," said Gwyneth to Isabella, "and this gentleman with him is his son, Andrew."

"A pleasure to meet you," said Andrew in a voice that bore a natural softness, a trait well suited to his hoped-for situation in the clergy and which, in the present circumstance, added a sense of warmth to his greeting. "My father has spoken most highly of you, and as you have already made friends with someone as esteemed as Miss Gwyneth, I can conclude that he is correct in every detail." As he straightened from his courteous bow, he continued, "And please allow me to introduce my friend Carlton Garrick. Carlton is a very talented artist, and someday I shall be very proud to say I knew him before he was famous."

"Which is to say," added Carlton, "while he was yet poor and undiscovered and having no advantageous attachment to anyone."

The camaraderie was infectious, and amongst these few people already inclined to enjoy the evening, Isabella began, perhaps for the first time since her arrival from Spain, to think herself truly among friends. In that spirit, she was just on the point of taking notice of the particular attention Gwyneth was paying to the young artist when Andrew interrupted her observations with, "But what are we thinking? This night is made for dancing, and here are two charming ladies standing. My skills cannot be said to be polished, but, Miss Isabella, if you would do me the honor of the next dance, I shall be very glad to try my utmost to be your most respectable partner."

The delight in Isabella's eyes was all the answer that was needed, but Isabella's enthusiastic, "Oh, yes, yes, indeed," left no doubt that a dance would be most welcome. With scarcely more than an exchange of nods, Carlton and Gwyneth eagerly joined them in their procession to the dance floor.

The dance was a duple minor, newly designed as a longways set and rapidly becoming a favorite among the more progressive members of the gentry. It was cleverly designed and had in its measured steps, as was common to most country dances, certain aspects that were sympathetic to the egalitarian attitude that was increasingly evident in Europe. It was the fraternization of the couples that made it so, for if one chose to view it as such, the dancers had two roles to portray: primary couples, who could be considered to act as the gentry, and secondary couples, who might be considered servants because of their supportive role to the gentry. Inevitably, as the dance progressed through its various movements, members of the upper and lower classes ultimately traded roles, the first becoming last even as the last became first, as had also been known to happen in Europe.

Of greater importance to the younger dancers, though, was the opportunity to smile pleasingly, to tease, and perhaps to flirt charmingly, not to mention the occasion for gloved hands to touch or the chance to glimpse a shapely ankle in the performance of a rigadoon step. Isabella addressed the dance admirably with youthful zeal, while Andrew, with evident pleasure and more simple skill than elegance, acquitted himself handsomely.

Had the evening been brought to a close at that precise moment, Isabella and Andrew might scarcely have noticed. Others, however, were not so enamored of the progressive engagements that had been nudged, be it ever so gently, into the beginning of the ever-so-slow precipitation of social evolution. It is, indeed, one of the misfortunes of society that the presence of happiness in one part is often viewed with suspicion by those of another quarter who view it from afar. That is to say, envy invariably compels the latter to diminish the good fortune of the former. In practiced society, where it is easier to capture the attention of others with unkind remarks than with polite discourse, this diminution is done by the wagging of malicious tongues. In the present circumstance, the unpopular plan to restore Southjoy Mission, the upheaval of local social order by the arrival of Lady Sylvia, and the elevation to social prominence of a stranger of no apparent fortune was stimulus enough for many sharp tongues. Of course, within the rules of engagement in a rigid social structure, few tongues would long wag, should they choose to disparage in any respect a person of the stature of Lady Sylvia. But of Isabella, a mere ward with no connections, save for a nearly unacknowledged relationship to Lady Sylvia, much prevarication could be achieved unreservedly by scarcely shaded innuendo.

"Do my eyes see correctly?" asked Mrs. Krumsuch of Mrs. Droutsworthy. "Is that not Mr. Cunnings's son dancing with Miss Isabella? He is a rather common fellow, is he not? Could it be that no proper gentleman has asked her to dance?"

"Mr. Cunnings has been retained by Lady Sylvia, you know," replied Mrs. Droutsworthy. "He is quite respectable in his profession, as I have heard. I do not doubt that his employment entails a certain, shall we say, obligation toward Lady Sylvia's charge, the poor child being one of Lady Sylvia's more charitable affairs, as I understand it. As to the son, well, a proper son owes duties to the father. I think I need say no more."

In the center of the tearoom, situated beneath the central chandelier of three, a spaciously elegant table had been prepared exclusively for Lady Sylvia. There, with the expected retinue of servants and attendants arrayed behind her, sat Her Ladyship and, across from her, Miss Ariana Atwood.

"Unless I am much mistaken, and I never am," said Lady Sylvia, "you are much astonished by my invitation."

"I must admit that I had no prior thought of such a privilege," replied Ariana, as yet uncertain of her position.

"Nonsense," declared Lady Sylvia. "You may equivocate in polite discourse with others, but I beg you, please, do not speak to me any pretense. I am too well versed in them all, and I am pleased by none of them. You are astonished at my invitation because a person of your station has absolutely no expectation of any attention from me whatsoever."

"Well," said Ariana yet with some hesitation, "I admit that I was, and am, astonished by your interest, that I had no expectation of your attention, and further, that I am, even now, ignorant of the reason for my presence and your interest."

"Thank you, my dear," said Lady Sylvia with apparent satisfaction. "The firmness and clarity of your response is precisely what I," said Her Ladyship with a firm emphasis on *I*, "expected of you." She paused to address a gently pleased look upon Ariana and then continued, "Yes, expected, for I have always required of myself to be versed in the character of those who might have cause to petition me or generally be in my company. Would it surprise you," she asked with genuine interest, "that certain acquaintances declare you to be 'headstrong'?"

"I cannot deny such a report," replied Ariana cautiously before adding with some degree of resigned humor, "when I have been the direct recipient of that characterization myself."

Lady Sylvia offered a satisfied nod towards Ariana. "I congratulate you on your forthright answer, and now, I, too, shall be forthright with you." She paused to collect her thoughts and then continued in the same manner.

"As you no doubt have surmised yourself, I am not a helpless, grieving widow. I am, rather, a determined, loving widow who will honor her husband's memory by seeing his vision of Southjoy Mission completed as he so often described it to me. I am, also, not insensitive to the fact that Southjoy Mission does not enjoy great favor among the local inhabitants. I intend to bridge the conflict between Sir Waverly's wishes and local inhabitants' apprehensions."

Lady Sylvia glanced with some satisfaction at the quizzical look that had gathered across Ariana's brow. She continued, "To do that, I shall need an assistant of good sense and good character who will speak to me what needs to be spoken, and without reservation."

Ariana's thoughts swirled in a state of flux as she considered what Lady Sylvia might reasonably intend by revealing this prospectus of her personal affairs to one such as herself, who, by comparison to Lady Sylvia, was of unexceptional station.

"Additionally, the person who assists me must also serve as a reliable liaison with local inhabitants, someone they would trust and respect, and who could make such local arrangements as may be necessary for our progress."

As the frown upon Ariana's brow deepened, Lady Sylvia leaned slightly toward her, her countenance coming to bear fully into Ariana's own focused, if uncertain, regard of Her Ladyship.

"I have researched the matter most carefully, and I believe," said Lady Sylvia with unreserved confidence, "there is none to be found more suitable to my purpose than yourself, you, Miss Ariana Atwood."

In the mundane course of even the most ordinary lives, there are moments of such unexpected import that they defy instant comprehension. This surely was one such moment for Miss Ariana Atwood, whose expression had become a study in perplexity.

"I have a further reason for addressing you in this manner," said Lady Sylvia. "I believe it would serve young Isabella well to have a companion closer in age to herself than myself." Observing Ariana's expression evolving toward a look of interest or at least curiosity, Lady Sylvia added, "In that regard, let me hasten to observe, lest it should be a concern to you, that you need not fear that Isabella might feel awkward in English society. Indeed, since early childhood, she has had the advantages of both an English governess and a Spanish governess, and you may find on occasion that she is more English in her manners than are we."

She again paused, allowing Ariana an opportunity to blink her eyes.

"In return," continued Lady Sylvia, "if you agree to this petition, you shall reside at Southjoy Mission for as long as may be required, and you shall enjoy the privileges of such an association. Indeed, it shall be your responsibility to entertain visitors there, with or without my own attendance, which shall afford you an introduction into the finer circles of society and respectability and might even accord you a more favorable match than you might otherwise have opportunity to expect."

Lady Sylvia then looked contentedly upon Ariana still absorbing what she had just heard, whereupon Her Ladyship concluded, "I believe this to be a fair bargain. I know you shall wish to discuss it with Mr. and Mrs. Atwood. I leave that interview to your discretion, and I shall await your reply, as soon as may be possible, at Southjoy Mission."

And with that, tea was concluded, Lady Sylvia turned her attention once again to the multitude of guests who had come to honor her, and Ariana hurriedly departed through the adjoining Octagon Room in search of her sister, Gwyneth, who must be the first to hear of this astounding proposition.

Chapter 3

As was to be expected, Mrs. Atwood was ecstatic at Ariana's news, while Mr. Atwood mounted strenuous opposition, declaring the very idea to be abhorrent to his peace and deriding the incumbent loss of the very solace he derived from the person of his eldest daughter. Gwyneth understandably was stricken with anxiety at the prospective distancing of her sister, who was also her sole confidant, but was instantly relieved and even elated by Ariana's resolve to accept the offer on the condition that Gwyneth accompany her. As was to be expected, one man's brace could not withstand the force of three determined women, and in short order, Mr. Atwood surrendered to their will.

The modified terms of the arrangement were readily agreed to by all, with the exception of Mr. Atwood, whose sorrowful aspect nearly halted all discussion of the prospects. Ultimately, Mr. Atwood rallied himself and confirmed the undeniable benefits to be enjoyed by his daughters. In less than a fortnight, arrangements for the Miss Atwoods to be domiciled at Southjoy Mission were completed.

Another fortnight passed as the Miss Atwoods were introduced to and became familiar with the accommodations and the staff of Southjoy Mission, what modifications were anticipated by Sir Waverly's plan, and what was suitable now and what was yet required for the proper entertainment of visitors. As they explored the mansion, Ariana frequently wandered from room to room, pausing here and there to examine details of pedestals and wall hangings, often standing pensively for long periods of time. She did this most particularly in the large sitting room where her eyes would slowly pan the old tapestries that adorned the walls. Though they were worn by age and insects, she hoped some could be preserved. They added greatly to the sense of warmth that pervaded this part of the mansion. Indeed, throughout Southjoy Mission, Ariana experienced a feeling of welcome, not merely because she already shared with Lady Sylvia the kind of attachment one admires in the closeness of mother and daughter, but also because the ancient mansion itself seemed to exude a charm that reached outward especially to her. In Ariana's perceptive eyes, the charm she beheld was melded into appreciative observations that she expressed frequently to her sister. "You are smitten!" Gwyneth had teased. Ariana paused only slightly before replying softly and simply, "I feel that I belong here." Her words bore such sincerity that Gwyneth found herself regarding with some surprise the look of contentment that encompassed Ariana's unguarded continence. "Smitten, but in a true and honest way," said Gwyneth quietly as she watched Ariana close her eyes wherein she might allow her newest impressions to be formed into an indelible memory that she would bear most fondly in her thoughts.

The impressions of both Ariana and Gwyneth were conveyed in frequent notes to their mother. Their letters quickly became a commentary on the delights they had discovered or the amusing mishaps that had befallen them in the course of their day. Gwyneth wrote volumes about Miss Isabella, whom she praised unreservedly, while Ariana was conscientiously discreet in her praise of Lady Sylvia, to spare Mrs. Atwood the twinge of envy that might otherwise be occasioned by such praise, and devoted the larger part of her communications to the wonders of Southjoy Mission. Mrs. Atwood inevitably replied with a lengthy discourse on Mr. Atwood's contrariness in the absence of their daughters, within which, however, the daughters could readily perceive their mother's own doleful moods. Yet, every letter, whether written by mother or daughter, concluded with expressions of encouragement and hopeful prospect.

A further opportunity to explore the property in its entirety arose when Lady Sylvia, accompanied by Isabella, made a brief excursion to Bath to finalize certain financial arrangements that would facilitate the anticipated renovations of Southjoy Mission.

Gwyneth, perhaps because she was the more impressionable, was most enchanted by the large banquet room that could not only host a large feast but could also serve as a very fine ballroom. The perimeter of the room was set off from the main floor by a series of arches and columns, three arches along each side and two across each end. These archways were very suitable for socializing and promenading, while the main floor, cleared of tables and chairs, would provide a spacious area for dancing.

Ariana, in contrast, felt herself drawn to the library, where picturesque shadows reached out to cross the room at odd angles while an odor of old leather wafted from the shelves lining the room. She turned slowly through the room, finding therein a strange curiosity beginning to tug at her thoughts. Large numbers of books, very old books, stood prominently on the shelves sheltered by the deepest shadows, books whose bindings were deteriorating, cracking, straining to retain who knew what wisdom, what secrets. Her fingers lightly caressed the titles as though she might sense by her touch what her eyes could no longer read upon the worn covers. The oddest of the ancient volumes was a small book, oddly small amidst other, more substantial volumes, and plain whilst the others were adorned with gilded letters, which, though now illegible, gave them greater prominence. The oddity itself caused her to pause. Its plainness bid her hand to reach beyond the other volumes, to gently pull it away from its towering neighbors, and to cradle it in her hands as though it were a frail but precious relic. Holding back her breath with a sense of near reverence, she parted the covers to reveal, preserved yet on flaking pages in carefully hand-lettered script, an apparent title:

The True and Rite Hiftorie of the Herefie of Edmund Plagyts.

Below the title, farther below, near the bottom of the page in smaller print, in less careful, oddly frenetic and wavering lettering: "Let nun read these paiges who have feer of euil."

Stung with alarm, Ariana slammed shut the covers of the book and, in but a single motion, placed—nay, stuffed—the book onto the shelf, leapt to the floor, departed the room, and took not a further breath until the afternoon sun in the small garden atrium fell warmly upon her face. Flushed with a tumult of mixed emotions, Ariana could only stand and wait as Gwyneth came quickly to her from the garden bench on which she reposed when Ariana burst upon her solitude.

"Ariana, what is it?" she exclaimed. "What has happened? Speak, I beseech you! Why are you so agitated?"

Ariana gestured with her hand, for she could not yet speak and had need of gathering her thoughts to assure herself that what she had seen was real and not imagined, that she had been there in the library, that she had seen…what, a book? Yes, a book, but a book that might hold the secret of the curse that had enshrouded Southjoy Mission for centuries.

Chapter 4

The following day held little opportunity for speculation or the exploration of unexpected curiosities by inquisitive minds, for Lady Sylvia returned from Bath with news of the imminent arrival of her nephew, Mr. Cedric Stacey. All must be made ready, from stables to bed chamber, from light refreshments to hearty supper, and all must be made presentable to the discerning eye of that estimable gentleman. Lady Sylvia was adamant on this point, that Cedric's introduction to Southjoy Mission should occur without inconvenience to him. His good opinion must be secured from the very first moment.

Mr. Cedric Stacey, whose opinion was so valued by Lady Sylvia, had remained something of a mystery to the greater part of the local inhabitants. The most that anyone would venture to say was that Mr. Stacey was considered "distant" and "aloof." Such, at least, was the opinion of those who only knew him indirectly, which is to say, not at all.

Closer acquaintances, however, fully agreed that such a trait was indeed a prominent attribute of Cedric's character; his manner often was unapproachable and impersonal, even to those who knew him well. It must be assumed that it was a role that suited him, for he was long familiar with it. His mother had died at a young age giving birth to his sister, who, though younger than himself, might well have given Cedric a different focus on life if she had not died of influenza in her infancy. Likewise, neither his father nor his older brother contributed much to his formative years, his father having died undistinguished in the service of the crown and his brother perishing in a mishap at sea. Were it not for his uncle, Sir Waverly, the existence of Cedric Stacey might well have gone unnoticed by the world at large.

Sir Waverly had no children of his own, and when he learned that Cedric was to be adrift without the care and attention of family, he took charge of Cedric with the same passion he addressed to any of his prized enterprises. It was under Sir Waverly's tutelage that Cedric learned to abhor the frivolous, to champion a cause if it but advanced his or his neighbor's dignity, and to oppose vigorously abuses of any nature. It is probable that the success of this tutoring accounted for the manner in which Cedric seemed to be untouched by the tragedies that surrounded him.

At university, Cedric distinguished himself handsomely, though not brilliantly. He had a fine mind for organization but little in the way of insight or common sense. His thoughts were deliberate and deductive, and though somewhat ponderous, he could usually see his way through the most puzzling of problems, given sufficient information and time. Materially, he wanted for nothing, thanks to Sir Waverly, who, however, was careful to provide only a sufficiency for modest expenditure. More privileged students, who seemed invariably unsuited to academic life, often were envious of his accomplishments and would have disdained him were it not for his connection to Sir Waverly. When these latter personages, with a view to an acquaintanceship with Sir Waverly, attempted to ingratiate themselves by means of hollow platitudes, Cedric curtly rejected them. In consequence, Cedric had few friendly associates and might have been shunned entirely had it not been for one particularly unpleasant affair that transpired midterm in his second year.

It seems a middling student, Mr. Gavin Raith, had managed to offend several fellow students of the privileged class. Having been orphaned early in his life and raised by a competent tradesman, he could boast of no advantage for himself save for his own cleverness. That was cause enough for him to be subjected to the disdain and ridicule of his wealthier fellow students, to whom he responded by taunting them with their own ignorance. At midterm, one of the more hapless of those privileged students was attempting to cheat on an exam, but unfortunately, a slip of paper on which certain answers had been scribbled fell to the floor during the exam. The proctor espied it almost instantly. When the latter good fellow demanded the identity of the person to whom the incriminating paper belonged, many fingers unhesitatingly pointed to Gavin Raith. Cedric, however, had witnessed the incident and defended Gavin vigorously. On careful examination of the incriminating paper, Cedric observed that one of the answers was quite incorrect. Suspecting that Gavin knew better, Cedric suggested a review of Gavin's examination book, which quickly revealed that Gavin had answered the question quite differently and quite correctly. To the chagrin of the majority of his classmates, Gavin was fully exonerated. From that moment on, as many would note, Gavin Raith was Cedric Stacey's devoted friend.

At first, Cedric felt an obligation not to abandon Gavin or to reject his overtures of friendship, but he was soon genuinely won over by the charm of Gavin's ready wit and his unconcerned attitude regarding any event surrounding him. This camaraderie, however, was cause for further social irritation, and it was not long before a certain tongue began to wage a campaign of innuendo to injure the reputation of Cedric Stacey by way of revenge for his aloofness and his defense of an "unsuitable" student, namely Gavin Raith. Cedric was inclined to demonstrate his superiority by ignoring the gossip entirely, even though it was certainly slanderous. Gavin, however, was not so inclined. Having once been befriended by Cedric as by no one ever before, Gavin assumed an attitude of one wholly and fiercely loyal to his friend. Through one of his cleverest orchestrations, Gavin proceeded to swindle the unfortunate fellow who had had the audacity to promulgate the calumny against Cedric. This he did with such finesse and cunning that, if revealed, the humiliation of the student would have been unbearable. Indeed, the incumbent shame would risk a loss of inheritance for the young man. In consequence, the student bitterly accepted that no charges could be brought against Gavin without revealing his own foolishness, which his family might well interpret as unworthiness. Not to forego revenge, however, the victim, as he perceived himself, thought instead to damage Gavin's friendship with Cedric Stacey by confronting Cedric privately with a profusion of indignant outrage. It was to no avail, however, as Gavin readily acknowledged his role and even justified it as a matter of honor and self-respect. Cedric was inclined to accept Gavin's explanation, for the student evidently had perceived sufficient fraudulence in his own conduct that the affair was to be terminated without further ado or publicity. A good while later, when Cedric and he had occasion to reminisce about the affair, Gavin commented that there was a certain utilitarian aspect to the matter as well, as the student's misguided intentions had helped to nullify certain debts that Gavin had accrued. Besides, offered Gavin, given that the student was of the weak and pathetic sort, there was in the affair a good lesson for him as well: for those from whom much can be taken, much is taken, and they must learn how to take back, else they may be set upon again and again. Though Cedric was not pleased with Gavin's cynicism or his method, the result, he had to admit, was rather satisfactory, and, in full fairness, it must be said that neither Cedric nor Gavin ever again suffered ridicule, by calumny or otherwise. It was a result that could be construed as a credit to Gavin if viewed rightly.

"Cedric, my dear nephew," declared Lady Sylvia, "how much I hoped you would visit before many changes were made in this wonderful mansion. I wanted you to see it as it is now, dark and brooding, and now that you have, I shall look forward to your return when it is handsome and proud."

"For my part, I have always considered it to be an adequate structure, albeit blemished by time," said Cedric with a sweeping gaze that took in the larger expanse of the entrance hall. "It is certainly far from the shrine to Sir Waverly that you would have it be, and far be it from me to deter any honor to that fine gentleman. He was good and civil toward me, and I begrudge him no recognition of his many merits."

Voices and the rustle of day dresses emanated from the adjoining parlor as the young ladies who occasioned them approached the new arrivals with apparent excitement and anticipation.

"And now, nephew," said Lady Sylvia in a lightly formal but pleased tone, "allow me to present to you your cousin, Miss Isabella de la Vega, and with her, my new associate, Miss Ariana Atwood, and her sister who accompanies her here, Miss Gwyneth Atwood.

"Ladies, I present to you my nephew, Mr. Cedric Stacey, and his friend Mr. Gavin Raith."

The latter gentleman, of slender build and rather smaller than Mr. Stacey, pointed his dimpled chin toward the ladies and smiled broadly in their direction. As he bowed at once to the ladies, his sparkling eyes seemed to address each of the young ladies individually, like a mutual confidant with a delicious secret that only he and she shared. Mr. Stacey, in contrast, tall and stately in bearing, acknowledged the ladies with only a slight nod of his head, the least that was formally acceptable, and while the ladies curtsied gracefully, Gwyneth leaned to whisper into Ariana's ear, "It's him, the rude gentleman who accosted us at Sydney Hotel!"

Ariana turned her regard from Mr. Raith to look more closely at Mr. Stacey. In the manner of courteous discourse for those newly introduced, she asked pleasantly of Mr. Stacey, "But, surely, you were here not long ago when the ball in Lady Sylvia's honor was held in Bath?"

"I came only so far as Bath on that occasion," replied Mr. Stacey. "I was summoned to London almost at once and so departed without the opportunity to visit the properties here, though I had seen the exterior some while ago." His manner suggested that he regretted neither the missed opportunity nor the tiresome company that would likely have accompanied that task. "Indeed, I would not be here now were it not for the kind entreaties of Lady Sylvia and the relentless insistence of my friend, Gavin, here, who assured me that good country air possesses restorative powers no city air can afford."

"Then how very fortunate for us that you have such a friend," said Lady Sylvia.

Before Mr. Stacey could reply and before Mr. Raith could modestly protest that it was his own good fortune to have such a friend, a servant arrived with tea, whereupon the company redistributed itself more congenially and settled into further polite discourse.

Gavin took this opportunity to stand next to Ariana, who sat somewhat on the edge of a straight-backed settee.

"Such a remarkable architecture," he said with an appreciative smile and the relaxed gesture of one who appreciates fine architecture. Lifting his gaze toward the ceiling and turning to follow the perimeter of the room, he asked with sudden interest, "I suppose there is a prodigious library?" He turned again to look at Ariana. "These old mansions often have the most wonderful libraries filled with ageless wisdom and, some say"—here Gavin paused to add a hint of conspiratorial interest—"hidden treasures!"

"Treasures?" beamed Miss Isabella, who sat next to Ariana. "Do you really think there could be a treasure hidden among the books?"

"I do not know about hidden treasures," replied Ariana with apparent amusement, "unless, of course, Mr. Raith means the rich thoughts and sentiments that fill the books. As to being prodigious, I can but say it is certainly the finest library I have ever seen."

"Then you have explored it in some detail?" asked Gavin.

"I have had but small opportunity to peruse its volumes," answered Ariana.

"And was there no one volume that caught your particular attention," asked Gavin with mock disappointment, "an unusually handsome binding, or perhaps a book left open where it was mysteriously abandoned before a reading could be completed?"

"No, nothing of that sort," said Ariana, suddenly pensive.

"Ah, but there was something," said Gavin with growing interest. "I see it in your eyes."

"Well, yes, there was something," said Ariana reluctantly, adding quickly, "It was nothing really."

"A mystery then!"

"No, not a mystery. More nearly an oddity. It was just that it was a small volume, old and out of place, you see, insignificant compared to the books around it."

"You intrigue me, Miss Atwood! Your mouth proclaims an oddity, but your eyes and demeanor betray something deep enough to furrow your brow. You must straightway reveal it to me! I sense you are a damsel in distress, and I must hie me to your rescue. I shall insist upon it!"

Ariana was instantly chagrined and bemused by the contrast of his levity and her own somber memory.

"Well," said Ariana with only the slightest hesitation, "perhaps Lady Sylvia would enjoy a few moments alone with her nephew? If so, we could adjourn to the library, and you could ascertain for yourself," she said in good humored challenge, "whether or not it is a prodigious library and its books in any way odd. Lady Sylvia, might that be agreeable to you?"

"Yes, that would do very well," said Lady Sylvia, speaking from across the room. "Miss Atwood already knows Southjoy Mission with a greater intimacy than even I, and she can provide you with a most encompassing tour. So if you young ladies would be so kind as to oblige Mr. Raith in this manner, I shall be happy to spend the time discussing more mundane, but necessary, business matters with my nephew."

When the others had left the room, Lady Sylvia turned to ask, "And now, Cedric, now that you have a first impression of Southjoy Mission, tell me plainly what you think of my undertaking. Is it foolish, do you think?"

Though she attempted to speak in a lighthearted manner, the timbre of her voice betrayed a hint of tension and concern, more that Cedric might not, in private, approve her project than that she might have overestimated her own abilities. Of her own capacity, she was quite confident. But the pragmatic Mr. Stacey might not see the merit of a posthumous homage of such extent and of such expense.

"It will require a considerable enterprise, that is for certain," said Mr. Stacey with due thoughtfulness, "and one that will take more than a little time in the doing. As to foolish, I cannot name it such. You have a strong will and a sensible disposition, and if this is your wish, then you surely have my approval." He paused to smile warmly at Lady Sylvia before continuing. "I worry only that the exertion will be exceedingly tiresome and wearing."

"Just so," replied Lady Sylvia with perceptible relief. "That is why I enlisted Ariana as my aide. In truth, she will bear the greater part of the burden."

"In that respect, allow me to urge upon you a modest observance of caution," said Cedric, cautious in his own tone. "I know you to be a good judge of character, but I do urge you to remember that you are now surrounded by strangers, including even Isabella."

"I know you speak with only the most sincere interest, and I thank you for that sensible advice," replied Lady Sylvia in her most congenial manner. "Yes, they were all complete strangers when we first met, but I have had no occasion to doubt their loyalty to me, and my confidence in them grows daily."

With a rarely offered affectionate smile, Cedric raised his cup to salute Lady Sylvia's effort. "Then you have my unreserved approbation."

The library at this hour, though well lit, had not yet the full warming of the sun so that the air was slightly cool against the cheek.

"It's a bit like a mausoleum," said Gavin, upon first entering the room, knowing full well the ladies would object most strenuously, "all these books laid to rest, fading and decaying as do all things in the course of time."

"What a truly morbid thing to say!" rebuked Ariana. "Books bear the fruits of our knowledge and become, in their turn, the seeds of future wisdom."

"Ah," replied Gavin, seizing upon the opportunity to tease the ladies, "but if a man be 'deep vers'd in books and shallow in himself,' as Milton so aptly said, of what good are the books?"

"If a man be shallow of character," retorted Ariana, matching tease to tease, "I think it is not likely he has probed any book to great depth!"

"I beg your pardon, Miss Atwood. I did not mean to imply that reading was of suspect value but only that those who only read do not gain the full benefit of the experience that inspired the writing."

"Perhaps," continued Ariana, "but surely it must be allowed that books themselves are treasuries of knowledge."

"Besides," added Gwyneth, speaking somewhat softly and perhaps a little deferentially, "I think a woman derives more from a book than does a man. Men engage the world and write books about it, so when they read, it is, perhaps, more cursory. It is a rarity for a woman to engage the world in such a manner or such an extent as to write a book about it, so books to us are far more precious. We live in times where upheavals change not just boundaries but whole societies. We ourselves have customs and practices that are not requirements of nature but of man. So we may wonder if people elsewhere conduct themselves as we do. We may indeed wonder whether other cultures even value our customs as we do. Such things are important to the survival of our own society, and we learn those things, not from conflicts and engagements, but from books about how people live."

Gavin, standing erect to his full height, raised his hands in mock surrender and, with his dimpled chin raised slightly upward, nobly intoned, "I yield, ladies. I yield. I am properly censured, and I humbly yield to your properly book-laden wisdom and," he added with his most engaging smile, "to your infinite charm."

"Mr. Raith! You are incorrigible!" declared Ariana, while laughing in the general humor of the moment. "In one breath, you flatter us with your humility, and in the next, you mock us with your impertinence."

"You are, in every respect, correct," said Gavin, in his most formal posture, "and I offer you my most sincere apology," he added, now bowing his acknowledgment, "for not according you the full esteem that three such learned ladies warrant."

The yielding laughter of the assembled company was evidence that his manner had achieved its intended effect and that the good humor in which the excursion to the library had begun was yet intact.

Gavin turned then to face Ariana directly to ask, "But what of this mysterious book? Are we not to investigate this oddity of which you spoke so enigmatically?"

"We shall indeed," said Ariana with a hint of suspicion that was given lightly but which was only partly mocking, "though I am not fully persuaded that your interest is truly of sober inquisition."

The sound of these words, even as they parted from her lips, caused Ariana's mind to blanch. Was it not the very memory of the tattered volume that inspired her mind to lean upon such a word as *inquisition* at this very moment? She wavered in place while the others drifted into the room. The tardiness of Ariana being, however, quickly noted, their progress collectively stopped as they turned back to look at her standing yet near the entrance. Gone now was the last glimmer of lighthearted countenance that a moment before had graced Ariana's demeanor. Now she was a picture of distraction, posed as though suspended in disquieting thought. Across the room, the wooden leg of a chair scraped against the floor. Its echoing squeal died to silence nearly as quickly as it had arisen. Yet Ariana stood unmoved.

"Ariana?" spoke Gwyneth into the growing silence.

"Yes," replied Ariana, recalling herself to the present, "yes, I'm coming."

"Ariana, I pray you are not ill?" asked Isabella, whose empathy was in perfect synchrony with the sincerity of her alarm.

"My dear lady," said Gavin with a certain exaggerated bravado, "I hope you are not preparing to have a fit of the vapors."

"Certainly not!" Though she attempted to scoff at the comment, there was a certain lack of conviction in her tone. Recovering her demeanor quickly, however, Ariana explained, "I was just momentarily lost in thought." Walking across the room with a determined step, she stopped directly in front of the spot where first the book had captured her attention. "It is there," she said, pointing to the small volume that protruded slightly from its larger neighboring books.

The others gathered eagerly to her side to look keenly where Ariana pointed.

"It certainly looks meager enough," said Gavin, sounding somewhat disappointed in his tone. "Rather harmless, in point of fact," he complained but then quickened his tone as he teased, "but perhaps it is merely mundane in outward appearance only, a latent evil cloaked in common garb to disguise its true mischievous character."

As Ariana frowned her disapproval, Isabella stiffened. The alarm awakened in her by Ariana's hesitation upon entering the room now swelled to a vague and diffuse sense of foreboding. Suddenly far away, she turned to peer through the nearest window, accepting its comforting light.

"In my country," said Isabella, "there was a terrible time of many inquisitions and much suffering. Many people turned to spells to ward off the evil that seemed to be everywhere. The church was outraged by them and waged a holy war against their evil power. Then everyone, the good and the evil, lived in fear of torture and death."

"Isabella," said Gwyneth, "I am chilled by your account, but surely you do not think such things happened here at Southjoy Mission!"

"No, surely not here," she replied, perhaps a little too quickly and perhaps with a tinge of guilt that she may have offended her friends.

Gavin looked from one to another and, seeing that all were prepared to continue, squared his shoulders to stand to his full height. In a posture of cautious readiness, he extended his strong arm forward to grasp the small book firmly in his hand. He tugged at the book gently to remove it from its place on the shelf and slowly, carefully brought the book to a respectful distance in front of him and within the clear view of all. In the speechless silence that now filled the room, Gavin turned back the cover of the book to reveal what appeared to be the title of the book, hand printed in an elegant script. Breaking the silence, he read the title aloud, converting the early English to modern English as he spoke, "*The True and Right History of the Heresy of Edmund Plagyts.*"

Gavin's eyes scanned to the bottom of the page. He squinted at the wavering scrawl and then turned the book at a small angle to better read the script.

"Let none read these pages who have fear of evil."

Isabella silently caught her breath as she pressed her hands involuntarily to her mouth.

"Then it is the Inquisition," she said, barely above a whisper.

"No," replied Ariana firmly in response to Isabella's distress, "it was not the Inquisition, at least not as you know it." As she attempted to quell Isabella's distress, she added, "Sometimes the persecution of heresy resembled it, that's true, but a real Inquisition was never convened in England."

"Not formally convened," interjected Gavin with decidedly unhelpful sarcasm, "but let's say it was borrowed when it proved convenient to do so, as was done, if I remember my history correctly, in the unsavory affair of Jehanne d'Arc."

As Ariana censured Gavin with a scowl, Gwyneth placed her hand softly on Isabella's shoulder, interposing with, "But those things all happened very long ago. It was a different time." Her quiet voice and gentle manner combined to comfort her young friend far more effectively than Gavin Raith's insensitive comment.

"I know," said Isabella without inflection, "but it frightens me to think of it." Then turning away and saying, "Please excuse me," she departed the room.

The remaining three looked from one to the other trying to discern in their bearings and attitudes whether to continue or to leave off their investigation of this oddity that roused such distress and interest. Gavin, with the book still in his hand, broke the silence.

"Right, then," he said firmly, "who's for it?"

"Proceed," said Ariana, more resolute than confident.

Gwyneth nodded agreement, albeit not without conveying some reluctance in an appraising glance at Ariana. A sister knows when a sister in being stubborn, especially one such as Ariana who might be inclined to be stubborn when to be otherwise might suggest a weakness or lack of confidence. Ariana, though, now seemed to be focused, and clearly no argument would deter her from this moment.

With a confirming nod then, Gavin carefully turned the pages to the first entry and read:

> In the year of our Lord, 1503,
> before the judges stood he,
> and in witness thereof was I
> who doth make this testament.

"Certainly a ponderous beginning," said Gavin, but it was already enough to rouse their interest to a state of intense concentration. Gavin motioned wordlessly to Ariana and Gwyneth to arrange themselves in the two chairs that stood to one side of the room while he positioned himself and the diminutive book before them.

He frowned as he looked at the following lines.

"The next part seems to be just pages and pages of acclamations of offices and authorities and holinesses ascribed to the inquisitors."

Alarmed by Gavin's incautious turning of the pages, Ariana exclaimed, "Careful! I fear the pages must be quite fragile. We must not do them injury beyond what age has already inflicted."

Gavin, with mock concern, but more cautiously, proceeded to turn the pages more slowly, finding at length the charge:

> You who bear the name, Edmund Plagyts,
> accused are you of consorting with demons
> and of blasphemy,
> for by your hand was writ—
> "Beyond the stars am I, and the stones.
> In all things am I, and all nothingness.
> Primordial passion am I, sayeth he,
> Prophet of all that was, and is yet to be."

Gavin paused to search through the text. "Apparently, he denied everything, and they began the torture almost at once. This appears to be a summary:

> Moon and stars fled from scorching days;
> sun faded into weeping nights.
> Defiant was he and unbroken.
> When darkest stood the bleakness of the night,
> when nighthawk's screech was none as shrill
> nor piercing sharp
> nor raucous more than he that spake,
> then, neath beshuttered eyes, spake he—

"Perdition to ye all!"
"Perdition and a thousand plagues!"

"Ariana, you were right!" It was now Gwyneth who whispered earnestly. "It is the curse, the curse of Southjoy Mission!"

"No," said Ariana sharply, and perhaps more forcefully than intended, for she quickly lowered her pitch as she continued, "not of Southjoy Mission, surely. Surely it was meant only for the inquisitors who tortured him."

It was a somewhat heated defense of Southjoy Mission, and it gave momentary surprise to both Gavin and Gwyneth, who, for their part, turned a startled and slightly admonishing look upon Ariana, who, by then, appeared as much surprised as they. Chagrined at having raised her voice to Lady Sylvia's guest, she motioned apologetically for Gavin to continue.

"Well, yes, possibly," allowed Gavin with a show of superior generosity. But then, seizing on the moment of advantage, he continued firmly, "But listen to this:

A chill shook mine own true flesh,
a chill of devil's touch,
for I did see, there, his piteous fate
gnashing against a void of unfathomable depth.
His anguish countenanced the curse of his vengeance—
"My spilt blood shall be as venom to ye foes of my peace
and upon ye generations."

"Where spilt his blood," intoned Gavin, "there shall be his curse!"

Ariana turned a disapproving look upon Gavin, who responded by drawing himself up to his full height and raising his chin in a mockery of defiance.

"I shall not believe it," declared Ariana, undeterred by Gavin's challenge. "There is warmth and charm here," she said, as her gesture swept the room and encompassed somewhat the whole of Southjoy Mission, "a charm that no evil curse could sustain. No," she said simply, "I shan't believe it."

"But there is more?" asked Gwyneth.

"That seems to be the essence of the matter," replied Gavin. "The next passage might be a kind of closure:

> Upon the instant he did speak of menace,
> his spirit escaped his captors;
> no more the sufferance of shackles,
> no more the hold of torment.
> Thus was the guilt of Edmund Plagyts assured,
> for naught but guilt flees on the breath of such evil.

"And there you have it," concluded Gavin. "The rest seems to be a collection of circumstantial evidence like this one, 'He espied my wife of an afternoon, and the next morn, the hens laid not their daily issue of eggs,' and this one, 'The milk soured immediately he did pass.'"

"It is more than enough to be distressing," replied Ariana. "Please, I beseech you, put the book back where you found it."

"But no!" urged Gavin. "There are many more pages, and who knows what might be found? Perhaps there is evidence of a descendant who is yet among us." Here, Gavin lowered his voice and bore open his eyes as he slowly pronounced, "And bears the sins of his ancestors."

Ariana flushed with sudden anger.

"You wish for us to pry into someone's tortured past to derive entertainment at the cost of another person's distress? I cannot believe you would make such a suggestion, even in jest. It is admirable to read old books for the useful knowledge they bear, but I fear that is not your motive."

"Besides," intruded Gwyneth, eager to avert the broaching argument, "we have too long deprived Lady Sylvia of your company."

"Yes," agreed Ariana, collecting herself and acknowledging Gwyneth's sensible attitude, "we have diverted you overly long, and perhaps," she added, "perhaps it is all just superstition anyway, the evidence and the curse alike."

Unwilling to yield, Gavin insisted, "The evidence, perhaps, but surely not the curse. You have heard it, 'the breath of evil.' No," said Gavin with growing exaggeration, "we must flee at once! You must away with me immediately and dwell in my protection!"

"Oh, do not make jest of it," pleaded Gwyneth with apparent apprehension. "The injury and suffering have been all too real, even if in the distant past."

Determined not to be denied his sport, Gavin declared, "If we are not to flee, then there is nothing for it but to straightway discover the nearest fire wherein to burn the bearer of this evil story!"

"No!" cried Ariana. "No, it must be preserved. What it purports as evidence of evil is no less than evidence of the innocence of Southjoy Mission. It shows that Southjoy Mission has been sadly shorn of it dignity, not by a curse, but by the self-inflicted fears ignorant people have created for themselves." More softly then, she continued, "Please, put it back on the shelf where you found it. Let that be its resting place and its shelter for yet a while longer."

Reluctantly, Gavin did as requested, though he was clearly not pleased with this outcome. In his estimation, it was Miss Ariana Atwood who had ultimately seized the advantage here. She had not succumbed to his charm and, therefore, must be lacking in warmth of spirit; had convictions too strong and, therefore, was lacking in feminine demeanor; and had frailties too few to be amenable to finer society.

Chapter 5

In the aftermath of the expedition to the library, Gavin and Ariana observed a mutual truce if not a pact of peace. Their conversations were politely congenial and only infrequently curt. Gavin gravitated to Isabella, paying particular attention to her, both in flattery and favor, and making a considerable show of delight whenever Isabella should enter a room.

Ariana, for her part and at the direction of Lady Sylvia, took every opportunity to engage the views and opinions of Cedric. Lady Sylvia was most anxious that her nephew be pleased with her grand undertaking, and though he admonished her nothing, she feared it was more politeness and respect than true endorsement. With Ariana, perhaps he would be more blunt and factual, there being no need or occasion for him to be reticent or deferential. Hence Lady Sylvia instructed Ariana to be unsparing in her attention to Cedric.

Ariana accepted this assignment with enthusiasm and began at once her campaign to win Mr. Stacey's approval. Her exhibition of plans and ideas flowed with a natural exuberance that was wholly free of self-conscious inhibitions.

"We have had a thought to convert the small parlor room into a gentleman's room, but we are uncertain whether or not such a room would appeal to a gentleman's perspective."

"I would venture that it is a most excellent idea. Gentlemen have a greater inclination to pampering than they are inclined to admit. I think the notion would become more fully appealing, however, if you would consider changing the wall covering to something less delicate than at present," offered Mr. Stacey.

"And the furniture?"

"Something more rugged, I should think."

"A gaming table, too, perhaps?"

"Yes, most certainly, Miss Atwood. Lady Sylvia was quite correct when she said you have a quick mind." Ariana blushed only slightly as Mr. Stacey smiled pleasantly at her before adding, "If other matters of similar question should arise, I would be pleased to offer you such advice as may prove useful to your project."

"I am most grateful," replied Ariana warmly, accentuating her reply with the warmth of her own smile.

As they continued in this manner, Lady Sylvia felt a certain contentment as she observed how attentively Cedric listened to Ariana's discourse and how readily he responded with opinions when Ariana sought his views. On several occasions, he offered suggestions of his own, which Ariana eagerly noted.

The amity and the exceptional facility with which Ariana and Cedric worked together that day prompted Isabella to remark rather coquettishly, "I think you have a liking for Mr. Stacey, no?"

"I think he is a most worthy gentleman," replied Ariana, rather objectively. "Lady Sylvia has high regard for his views on these and, indeed, on all matters, and I too have come to value his opinion."

"He is a handsome man, I think," said Isabella. "I have heard even the servants say he is very handsome."

"I believe he is considered so," said Ariana, not wishing to continue this train of thought.

"He is admired greatly by Lady Sylvia, don't you think?" asked Gwyneth.

"Most certainly. She could want for nothing more excellent by way of a nephew," agreed Ariana.

"And you are admired by Lady Sylvia too. I have heard her say so," added Isabella.

"I am grateful for her confidence," acknowledged Ariana.

"Then," asked Gwyneth playfully, "since you are admired by Lady Sylvia, and Mr. Stacey is admired by Lady Sylvia, and both of you admire her, does it not follow that you two should admire each other also?"

"Really, Gwyneth," scolded Ariana. "That is too incorrigible to warrant reply."

On the following day, however, Mr. Stacey's attention seemed to waver with a preoccupation of another thought. When Ariana sought to clarify the matter of wall coverings for the gentleman's room, Mr. Stacey replied rather curtly, "I believe we discussed that issue rather thoroughly yesterday."

"Indeed, your thoughts were most concisely expressed," replied Ariana, "but I am most anxious that the room appear absolutely comfortable to a true gentleman like yourself."

It was, perhaps a rather fawning remark like many Mr. Stacey had encountered in other circumstances with annoying frequency, and yet, spoken by a simple country girl like Ariana, it could well be a genuine recognition of his superior station. Though perturbed by his own lack of certainty, Mr. Stacey chose to reserve his judgment on this thought for the moment. However, upon a similar repetition of this conduct on the third day, the effect of Ariana's incessant queries and petitions tipped the scale of judgment adversely. As Ariana commented once again on how much she valued his opinion, Mr. Stacey abruptly interrupted her rather rudely.

"Miss Atwood, shall we dispense with this pretense of civility?"

Ariana could but stand speechless for a moment so unexpected was this affront.

"I beg your pardon, Mr. Stacey," she pleaded. "Have I said something to offend you?"

"The offense is not in your words but in your conduct," accused Cedric with evident scorn.

Ariana stared at him, her face stung to a frozen blankness, her bearing breathless and rigid as her mind recoiled from this sudden and inconceivable condemnation of her character so brutally advanced.

"I beg of you," she managed to say scarcely above a whisper, "tell me in what manner I have offended propriety."

"Come now, Miss Atwood," chided Mr. Stacey. "Did you think to sway me with your feminine attentions? Then permit me to disabuse you of such notions. I am well aware that a young girl of meager fortune might aspire to better herself through a sympathetic acquaintance with a superior class."

"What?" asked Ariana, now stunned a second time by such a further improbable statement. "Me?" she ventured to question. "And you?"

As awareness began to creep through her dazed confusion, Ariana suddenly burst into an unrestrained and indecorous laughter with such spontaneity as can only be ascribed to the wholly unanticipated and bizarre situation now confronting her.

"You and I, a match?"

She paused just long enough to regain her composure.

"Such a romantic notion I can understand from Isabella or Gwyneth, but you?" Then, as she began to comprehend the full import of Mr. Stacey's declaration, her words became tinged with the heat of the offended.

"Is that truly how you see me?" she asked. "I, a meager girl, pursuing you, a superior being?"

Her bearing became very still and rigid as the sudden flaring of her anger caused her breathing to come in short and rapid breaths.

"Be assured, Mr. Stacey, there is nothing in heaven or on earth beyond your own conceit that could ever conceive such an arrangement!"

She clenched her jaw defiantly, and though her wit, now sharpened with anger, was prepared to say more, much more, she abruptly turned away, decisively prepared to depart. Then, hesitating for a mere second more, she whirled just as abruptly to face Mr. Stacey calmly and soberly.

"Out of respect for your aunt, whom I have come to admire unreservedly, I shall say nothing more on this subject, and I pray you have the courtesy to do likewise." Whereupon she did turn and depart, slowly and measuredly, albeit with the sudden appearance of tears—the tears of inexplicable injustice, of trust denied, of wrongful accusation—all surreptitiously gliding across the gentle rise of her cheek.

Chapter 6

The departure of Mr. Stacey and Mr. Raith a few days later transpired civilly, warmly on the part of Lady Sylvia and with appropriate deference on the part of Ariana, who avoided, as much as the situation permitted, looking directly upon Mr. Cedric Stacey. After much thought, Ariana had concluded that it was best not to allow Cedric's undeserved condemnation of herself to divert her attention from the tasks Lady Sylvia had set for her. She allowed that Mr. Stacey could easily have mistaken her diligence for ambition, seeing it, as it were, somewhat out of context. Consequently, the most forceful response that could be given to this situation, the very condemnation of Mr. Stacey's own indictment, would be to greatly exceed Mr. Stacey's expectations, as indeed women generally must do when subjected to the judgment of men.

For some days, Ariana immersed herself in the mundane demands of her duties, and some that were not hers, exerting herself as though driven by a broaching desperation. Try as she would, though, her mind turned repeatedly to examine the humiliation she felt in the words that came mercilessly from the lips of Cedric Stacey. They would not stop echoing in her mind, even though in the late hours of the night she conceived the most biting of replies, the most piercing of rebuttals that would humble the pride of that aristocratic gentleman. And if her self-recrimination wearied of this fantasy, she recalled the altercation with Mr. Raith in the library, now firmly enhanced by an exaggerated scorn that, no doubt, Mr. Raith gleefully shared with Mr. Stacey.

It was in this frame of mind at one of her quieter moments that the thought occurred to her that both situations had a common base: the perception that Southjoy Mission was unworthy of the effort being expended on it. The indictments heaped upon Ariana were merely a reflection of Mr. Stacey's true thoughts of Southjoy Mission, and the attitude of Mr. Raith would seem to substantiate that conclusion, for if Mr. Stacey thought otherwise, then Mr. Raith would not dare to belittle any aspect of the enterprise undertaken by Lady Sylvia.

This understanding caused Ariana some little anxiety, for if Mr. Stacey, who was inclined to support Lady Sylvia, thought as much, how much more intense would the opposition to Southjoy Mission be amongst the local inhabitants? Clearly they and Mr. Stacey must be made to see Southjoy Mission in a different light. Ariana felt herself enervated by this thought as it seemed to harmonize perfectly with the very challenge Lady Sylvia had anticipated in acquiring her as an assistant.

The afternoon had turned to heavy clouds, and the rain of a light drizzle had applied a layer of dampness over the countryside. Gwyneth had installed herself in the little sitting room adjacent to the atrium and there sat upon the small window seat, listlessly, absently peering out at the vacant garden bench next to the trellis that had become her favorite retreat in fairer weather.

"Are you so very far away?" asked Ariana quietly, as Gwyneth took no notice of her entry into the sitting room.

Gwyneth smiled self-consciously and sighed lightly before replying.

"I suppose I am," she said, still smiling. "I was thinking of Bath and how beautiful it was the last time we were there."

"And would the charm of a certain artist be adding to the beauty of those thoughts?" asked Ariana with a certain sparkle in her own eyes.

"Yes, perhaps," answered Gwyneth, trying not to smile too broadly.

"Well, then, if that be so, I have an idea that might be pleasing to you," said Ariana, with feigned indifference.

When Ariana did not immediately offer an explanation of what the idea was, Gwyneth looked insistently upon her sister in a pose that left no doubt as to the eagerness of her anticipation, albeit with a mildly implicit reprimand of Ariana's teasing contained therein as well.

"I have just spoken with Lady Sylvia, and she is delighted with the idea," continued Ariana.

"Which is?" asked Gwyneth, abandoning all hint of reprimand in her growing excitement, for Ariana would not tease in this manner were not some exceptional event about to occur.

"Well," said Ariana, collecting her thoughts as she had done for Lady Sylvia, "the physical restoration of Southjoy Mission requires only materials and craftsmanship. Those can be had readily so long as there are funds to pay for them. But making Southjoy Mission a place of beauty might be to no avail if the minds of people are predisposed to dislike it." She paused just long enough to allow Gwyneth to acknowledge her agreement with this assessment and then continued. "It seems to me, then, that what we must do and do as quickly as possible is change how people think about Southjoy Mission."

"And how are you going to do that?" asked Gwyneth.

"By giving them a chance to see Southjoy Mission differently, to see it more personally." She paused to allow the delight in her eyes to further entice her sister and then concluded, "To see all the passion and intimacy that an artist might see in it."

"An artist!" said Gwyneth eagerly, asking, "Carlton?"

"Yes, precisely," said Ariana with much warmth. "Carlton."

There was little difficulty in procuring the services of a young artist who previously enjoyed no particular patronage, especially when the commission would place him in close proximity to the person he most wanted to be near. The commission itself was intriguing because it demanded a keener vision than any casual observer would have. Could, indeed, a place, any place, regardless of its construction, be made to radiate the spirit of the people who championed it? For Carlton, that was the essence of art, and he was prepared to immerse himself into the effort.

Gwyneth and Isabella eagerly accepted the proposition that they should serve as guides and aids to Carlton as he began to absorb and understand the vitality of Southjoy Mission. Ariana related the factual history of the estate and spoke at length about the rumors and hearsay that blighted the accounts of its history. She left it to Gwyneth and Isabella to conduct a visual survey of the estate and to show Carlton some of the more picturesque sites, along with those that, because of the mood they inspired rather than the picturesque quality of their settings, had become their personal favorites. Those sites, Carlton himself had remarked, were more appealing to him because, as he put it, "Mood is closer to the soul than to the facade."

After a thorough indoctrination of the premises, Carlton, the young man, reluctantly took leave of his guides so that Carlton, the artist, could begin the assimilation of his visual and cultural observations into sketches that might form the basis for the paintings that he hoped one day would be hailed as works of art. He worked rapidly in making numerous sketches of details—a window here, a nook there, the graceful arch of a tree limb. Using those, he proceeded more slowly to combine the elements into a whole that would portray something more than a physical presence. As his initial compositions began to take shape, he consulted Ariana as to their suitability.

"They are rather dark," noted Ariana.

"I suppose they are," replied Carlton, obviously disappointed by Ariana's response, "but they reflect what I see and feel."

Ariana sensed a certain defensiveness in Carlton's tone, and while Carlton was not particularly temperamental, she surmised that her remark was, perhaps, insensitive and that the situation now required her to continue in a more delicate fashion than she had begun.

"Forgive me, Carlton," she said softly but earnestly. "I fear I have expressed myself poorly. Your sketches admirably capture what Southjoy Mission has been in the past and what it is yet today. If I seemed disappointed, it was only because I am anxious for the world to see what Southjoy Mission could be one day in the near future, and if there is a fault to be acknowledged here, it is solely mine, for I have not yet found the words to impart that vision to you." She paused, momentarily deep in thought, and then continued with a sudden and promising brightness, "But I do have an idea."

Carlton, responding in kind with a smile halfway between tolerance and encouragement, replied, "I should be delighted to entertain it."

"I would like you to do a special sketch for me," said Ariana with growing enthusiasm, "before you do anything further."

"And what would be the nature of that sketch?" asked Carlton.

"A pleasant one, I think—my dear sister, Gwyneth. But," she hurried on, "not a portrait. I should very much like you to sketch her sitting on the corner bench in the little atrium garden."

Carlton brightened considerably at this request. He paused thoughtfully then said, "I see, yes. An excellent idea, that. If I focus on Gwyneth, I just might find a view of Southjoy Mission more in keeping with her spirit and, consequently, more as you would have it be."

"Yes, that is the idea exactly. And include all those lovely small details," added Ariana, "like the trellis in bloom and the adjacent window that looks into the sitting room."

Chapter 7

Lady Sylvia increasingly credited the progress made at Southjoy Mission to the good sense of Ariana, and it was on the account of that credit that Lady Sylvia approved the boldest of Ariana's suggestions made in the course of their latest interview.

"Lady Sylvia," Ariana had said, "if we are to win popular acceptance of Southjoy Mission, we must recognize that it will be a very long and slow process unless we address ourselves to the very heart of those who oppose it."

"You refer, no doubt, to the Society of Native Architectures and Gardens," said Lady Sylvia with some reluctance. "You realize, of course, Mrs. Crandesol is not only an ardent opponent of Southjoy Mission, but also, in my opinion, a person of considerable pettiness and, perhaps, even jealousy and who is more than a little covetous of the title conveyed to me by Sir Waverly's knighthood."

"Nonetheless," said Ariana firmly, "we cannot ignore her. Her position with the society affords her much influence. If it is seen that you, Lady Sylvia, have taken the initiative to approach her, the good will of that deference will be noted by all, regardless of the outcome of your petition."

"But is there not a possibility that a rejection would be seen as an embarrassment to the honor of Sir Waverly?"

"I cannot deny it," replied Ariana, "but there are many people who have suffered in one way or another at the indifference and arrogance of SNAG. The disfavor of Mrs. Crandesol may well stand you in good favor with the majority of those people who are greater in number."

Mrs. Crandesol had received Lady Sylvia's petition for an interview with neither surprise nor satisfaction. It was expected, and if there was a sense of incipient elation, it was that of a predator before whom the prey had suddenly appeared. Southjoy Mission had long been a festering sore to the Crandesol family. For whole generations, it had been assumed that the mansion would decay into oblivion. Yet, there it stood, year after year, defying deterioration, refusing to crumble. Her husband, a fool of a man, may he rest in peace, had failed in an attempt to destroy the mansion in an act of arson, in which he himself was injured before ever reaching the mansion. He subsequently died of an infection resulting from that injury. And now, Lady Sylvia would have it glorified, like a martyr raised to sainthood when others would have it dead and departed.

The reception of Lady Sylvia and Miss Atwood was decidedly unfriendly. Mrs. Crandesol sat stiffly with a scowl focused uniquely on Lady Sylvia. Behind her loomed the Crandesol family crest with its half-bird, half-lion figure stretching out its menacing talons as though they were reaching purposely toward Lady Sylvia in a merciless posture of attack. Ariana, who was completely disregarded by Mrs. Crandesol, sat next to Lady Sylvia, but separated from her by perhaps a yard, making it difficult to confer with each other should the occasion for such need arise. Mrs. Droutsworthy, who had joined Mrs. Crandesol for this interview, sat impassively somewhat behind Mrs. Crandesol where she was as much disregarded as was Ariana, though she took it upon herself to nod courteously to the visitors upon their arrival. Mrs. Crandesol had greeted them with no such cordiality and had been quick to exhibit an unsympathetic attitude even to Lady Sylvia's devotion to her late husband's memory. Her impatience with Ariana's rational presentation of the historical significance of Southjoy Mission was more than apparent.

"Southjoy Mission is a blot on our history and on the natural beauty of our countryside," rebuked Mrs. Crandesol sternly. "Good English countryside," she added with emphasis. "If you want my opinion, it should be burnt to the ground and its ashes spewed into the farthest sea."

"But that would only create a deeper scar," said Ariana, who could see that her opportunity to be reasonable was rapidly waning. "We cannot change what is already entrenched in history. Would it not be better to heal the wound and allow the beauty of its own natural innocence to flourish?"

"Natural innocence, you say? Southjoy Mission was the scene of vile corruption and even torture," said Mrs. Crandesol with contempt.

"But it was not the cause of either," retorted Ariana. "It was abused. It was the victim of vile people who craved after power and influence."

Mrs. Crandesol rose imperiously to her feet, projecting her most crimson image of fury upon Ariana, upon whom she looked for the first time since their arrival. "And because I have some influence in this shire," she cried shrilly, "you will next accuse me of being vile too, I suppose?" The wave of her hand conveyed the violence of her mood as she exclaimed most caustically, "Such impudence! You come seeking my approbation. You shall not have it! Neither shall you have my countenance. No, you shall have none of it, nor shall I warrant association with your project. I bid you take your leave this instant, for there is no welcome for you here." Whereupon, Mrs. Crandesol turned abruptly and departed the room, it being left unmistakably apparent that Lady Sylvia and Miss Ariana were to show themselves out.

Chapter 8

Gwyneth sat primly on the corner bench in the small atrium adjacent to the library. She found a certain measure of both pride and pleasure in watching Carlton as he worked. He was truly a skillful artisan, rendering swift and efficient movements of his hand into an engaging sketch of his chosen subject. As she was now sitting as the object of his attention, there was ample time for observation and appreciation. From time to time, she surreptitiously swayed her head and neck slightly to relieve the accruing tension stemming from her effort to maintain a good pose. In the present instance, though, a small sigh escaped her carefully held composure. Not entirely from reflex, Carlton echoed her sigh with one of his own. Pausing then to study his sketch, he sighed once more, not the reflexive sigh of empathy this time but the deeper sigh of discouragement.

"Perhaps we should stop for today," he said without enthusiasm.

Gwyneth watched him as he gathered his materials, watched his face as he glanced impassively at his work. To Gwyneth, who now knew his moods and manners remarkably well, there was something other than fatigue written in his features.

"Dear Carlton," she began, "there is a kind of sadness about you today. Is it merely fatigue," she asked, "or is there something else that burdens you?"

Carlton looked again at his sketches as he decided how to reply and then motioned toward them as though directing a servant to clear away the dirty dishes.

"The problem," he said, still trying in himself to understand the full nature of the problem, "is that my work here has not come to life. It does not inspire the viewer to see beyond the mere physical presence of a building, an old one at that. Ariana says my work is rather dark, and I fear she is being too kind. She was clearly disappointed."

Gwyneth placed her hand on Carlton's arm, gently laying her head against his shoulder as she did so.

"If she is disappointed," said Gwyneth thoughtfully, "perhaps it is because she has come to see Southjoy Mission as a victim, like someone wrongfully abused and left destitute." She straightened and turned to look at Carlton with a faint glow of excitement beginning to tint her eyes. "She said as much one day when we were in the library. There is a small book there that greatly disturbed her, and we were discussing it with

Mr. Raith. I don't think even she has realized it, at least not consciously, but ever since finding that book, her perception of Southjoy Mission has changed. I now firmly believe she has come to regard her position not so much as a duty to Lady Sylvia, but more as a devotion to Southjoy Mission. What she perceived in that book, the empathy that she felt in the wholeness of her being, is what she is now most desperately trying to envision in the images you create!"

With growing excitement, Gwyneth related the incident in the library, describing in detail how Ariana reacted with a mixture of apprehension and reverence and how she was especially unsettled by Mr. Raith's unrestrained, irreverent attitude toward the tragic events that took place at Southjoy Mission.

"It was as though Mr. Raith had offended her personally," concluded Gwyneth. "I think that's what she wants you to reveal in your paintings—not the remnant external deterioration of the building, but rather the internal suffering of unjust abuse."

Carlton was momentarily captivated by Gwyneth's intent expression. In an ever-deepening appreciation of her intrinsic qualities, he said most warmly, "I do believe sometimes you have in you the spirit of a sensitive poet. By all means, I think you must show me this book."

Chapter 9

A fortnight had passed since the interview with Mrs. Crandesol, and the unpleasantness of that event had subsided in the minds of both Lady Sylvia and Ariana. Routine had returned to their daily affairs, and Ariana was now preparing invitations to bring a small number of neighbors to Southjoy Mission for an evening of social entertainment. The sudden and unexpected arrival of Mr. Cedric Stacey, however, had cast the household into a mild urgency of organized turmoil. Everyone knew what was expected of him, but no one was prepared for it to be expected.

"My dear Cedric," said Lady Sylvia by way of hasty welcome, "you cannot imagine what pleasure it gives me to have you visit us again and so soon! But do please forgive me for the lack of proper ceremony. Unfortunately, we had no hint of your arrival until this very moment."

"Do not concern yourself, Lady Sylvia," replied Mr. Stacey somewhat stiffly. "I have not come on a purely social visit. Indeed, I have come to address a decidedly unsocial agenda."

"Indeed. Then do please address it without delay," said Lady Sylvia with evident concern and not a little astonishment.

"I shall," said Mr. Stacey in the manner he had rehearsed several times before his arrival. "A most disturbing rumor has been reported to me, a rumor that concerns most particularly yourself."

Lady Sylvia's widened eyes and elevated eyebrows keenly expressed the totality of her surprise as she urged Mr. Stacey in her most earnest bewilderment, "Pray, do continue."

"The rumor has it," began Mr. Stacey, who quickly interrupted himself to interject, "and forgive me if I seem brutal, but I must report the matter to you as succinctly as I received it." Squaring his shoulders to Lady Sylvia, he continued firmly, "The rumor has it that you have felt obliged to seek out and *beg*," his tone weighed heavily on the latter word, "beg for the approval of Mrs. Crandesol, a known paragon of disapprobation, and her Society of Native Architectures and Gardens; that she *refuted*," again he emphasized the word, "refuted your proposal in its entirety; and that you were forced, in consequence, to retreat in public disgrace. That, I believe, is the rumor distilled to its full essence."

"Dear me," said Lady Sylvia slowly, as she gathered her thoughts, "that does sound rather devastating.

How did you come by this rumor, if you don't mind my asking?"

"Mr. Cunnings had occasion to speak to me and asked my pardon to relate what he had heard from Mrs. Krumsuch, who is acquainted, I believe, with Mrs. Crandesol."

"I begin to understand," said Lady Sylvia. "I had anticipated some such gossipy prattle but nothing quite so vitriolic as what you have described. If I were to venture a guess," she said somewhat practically, "I should think that Mrs. Crandesol left the embellishment of the story to her confidant, Mrs. Droutsworthy. Mrs. Droutsworthy attended the interview and, no doubt, distilled her own edited version of what transpired and, in the natural course of events, communicated that version, filled with slanted half-truths ready to be misconstrued, to her friend, Mrs. Krumsuch, who, I fear, has a readier tongue than a wit. From Mrs. Krumsuch, it would not be long in reaching Mr. Cunnings."

Mr. Stacey listened to Lady Sylvia's response with the growing sensation that the firmness of his position had become slightly off balance and perhaps even unsupportable. "Then, if I follow you correctly," he said, still hesitant to dismiss the affair but ready to be relieved of it, "you deny the veracity of the rumor?"

"Certainly," declared Lady Sylvia. "I am no such fool, as well you know." She nodded her head affirmatively as she continued, "We did pay a visit to Mrs. Crandesol. That much is true. Ariana had the idea that—"

"Ariana?" interrupted Mr. Stacey with sudden emphasis. "This was her doing?"

"If by 'her doing' you mean 'she suggested that it might be advantageous to call upon Mrs. Crandesol,' then, yes, it was 'her doing,' and, I dare say—"

"I might have known," interrupted Mr. Stacey, his displeasure suddenly reignited and his tone infused with disgust. He turned and briskly marched from the room, saying, "Excuse me, Lady Sylvia. I would have a word with Miss Ariana Atwood."

"Cedric, wait!" called Lady Sylvia to the door that was already closing.

Ariana was contemplating the first completed sketches Carlton had made of Gwyneth in the atrium, assessing their suitability as an initial exhibit to a small number of guests who would soon be invited to Southjoy Mission when Mr. Stacey burst into the room.

"Miss Atwood," asserted Mr. Stacey with barely constrained anger, "it is my understanding that you are here to assist Lady Sylvia. Is that not true?"

Stunned as she had been once before by the aggressive nature of Mr. Stacey's sudden and wholly inexplicable expression of displeasure, Ariana could only take a confused step backward, asking in a tone of unmistakable trepidation, "Mr. Stacey?"

No further reply was to be allowed, however, as Lady Sylvia rushed into the room, closely trailing Mr. Stacey.

"Cedric," she called sharply. "Cedric! Listen to me! You have misunderstood! Ariana is blameless in this affair. Indeed, she is to be credited and not blamed!"

"Credited?" questioned Mr. Stacey, still seething. "Credited with your disgrace?"

"Not disgrace," said Lady Sylvia firmly but with enforced calm. "Indeed, we were fairly certain of the outcome. We knew that refusal was likely to be the only response Mrs. Crandesol was capable of pondering. But we also knew what could be gained in popular support, even by her refusal, and indeed, since that occasion, I have received several commendations supporting our effort, all urging us to disregard the ill opinion of Mrs. Crandesol. One," she added more lightly, "even suggested that the depth of her displeasure was a reliable measure of the elevation of our own worthiness."

Ariana, the ashen discoloring of her face beginning to recede, looked first to one then to the other as she began to understand the commotion and its disturbance. As Ariana prepared to offer her own observations and defense, she was forestalled by Lady Sylvia who firmly asserted her authority in apprising Cedric of the entire affair from its planning to its conclusion.

When she had finished her account and was satisfied that Cedric more properly understood the situation in its true context, she concluded her assessment of the incident by saying, almost woefully, "You may believe me unreservedly when I tell you it was like trying to explain shoes to barefoot cretins—they already had feet, so why did they need shoes?"

Ariana, sensing that she was now given leave to speak, added forcefully, "It was worse than deplorable. The more rational we tried to be, the less rational she became. When that woman chose to speak to us at all, it was in comments distorted with half-truths. She deliberately deformed the wholeness of the truth into something odious. I had never before believed that basically good people would so unreservedly substitute deceit and deception for honesty and cleverness, as I believe Mrs. Crandesol and her cohorts have done."

"I bear the same opinion," agreed Lady Sylvia, "and I, too, have the sense that Mrs. Crandesol is, at heart, a decent person, but she is driven by a bitterness I cannot fathom. What is most disturbing, what saddens me the most, is that they set forth their deceit and half-truths with such facility as must derive from practiced dishonesty. I simply cannot fathom their conduct in this matter."

Cedric had calmed somewhat and had acquired a more thoughtful pose as he absorbed Lady Sylvia's remark and offered an acknowledging nod.

"I cannot say that I would have approved your venture had I been informed of it, but neither shall I condemn it now in retrospect. It would be unfair of me now to say there was no opportunity for success, but I may insist," he said, casting a dark glance look toward

Ariana, "that the effort was misguided from its beginning. The consequences were ill thought out."

Ariana, unwilling to be chastised so easily, was preparing a reply, but Cedric was not to be interrupted. He continued, but in a milder tone that he hoped achieved a balance between sympathy and objectivity.

"I would go so far as to suggest that they were predisposed to the failure of your request because people of that class have an inherent, nearly hereditary, social prejudice that pits them against their superiors. What they too often perceive is that denial is the prerogative of their superiors, and they resent it. What is ironic is that they would readily reverse the roles if they could, and they do so when an opportunity such as this one presents itself." His ire momentarily rekindled at this thought, and he said harshly to Ariana, "You, of all people, should have known that instinctively."

Ariana could not contain the flinch that stung her face even as his words stung her pride.

The implication of his tone was clear: "You are one of them," it said, "one of those of a lower class, so you should have known, even did know."

Ariana, suddenly engulfed in the fatigue of futility, unable to mount a further defense, surrendered to her chastisement and offered but the subdued agreement, "I fear it is so."

For Cedric, her muted tone carried, if not an admission of imprudence, at least an acknowledgment that, yes, she should have known what would happen for, yes, she was of a lower social class. For Ariana, constrained now to look inward, there was sufficient cause to at least wonder if, in her privileged position, she had forgotten the conventions of class distinction, that a superior class might view exposure to ridicule more severely than ordinary people.

Ariana's reticence and apparent deference to Mr. Stacey was sufficient to allow a momentary truce to settle quietly across the room, and in the ensuing silence, a conclusion to the matter was understood. Not fully satisfied with the outcome of this interview but not wholly discontent either, Cedric took his leave of the ladies, albeit with a parting look of unsettled suspicion cast upon Ariana.

Chapter 10

The commotion in the household occasioned by the unexpected arrival of important visitors was not entirely disturbing for everyone. For Gavin Raith, who accompanied Mr. Stacey, it was an opportunity for amusement. In his view, people are never so unguarded as when they are distracted by turmoil, and in such circumstance, the slightest glimmer of opportunity is readily apparent to someone as well versed in opportunity as Mr. Gavin Raith was known to be. Indeed, while Mr. Stacey attended to his onerous family matter, Gavin was free to go in search of Isabella, who would welcome the attention of the handsome Mr. Raith and whose youthful exuberance might lead her to be delightfully indiscreet regarding the affair with Mrs. Crandesol that had been so exceedingly disturbing to Cedric.

His search was not arduous, for Gwyneth and Isabella, having been made aware of the arrival of the visitors, had installed themselves in the little sitting room where they could account themselves admirably to any social protocol that might arise, as it invariably should when there are visitors of note to attend.

Gavin paused in the entranceway to beam his most engaging smile upon the two young women as he was announced to them. Isabella's dark eyes sparkled with anticipation as she remembered Mr. Raith's particular attention to her during his last visit with Mr. Stacey. Gwyneth, who remembered the latter occasion less fondly than her young friend, intended to offer only her usual cordial welcome but found that she could not constrain the warmth of her smile as she observed Isabella's apparent excitement. Attention begets attention, and Miss Isabella was nothing if not receptive to attention. And vulnerable, as Ariana would later remark to Gwyneth.

"Ladies!" he announced with a deep bow and a wide flourish of his hand. "I have the good fortune to be at your complete disposal should you be at liberty to welcome my humble presence."

"You are most welcome, Mr. Raith," said Gwyneth pleasantly, "and we shall gladly engage the pleasure of your company."

After the usual pleasantries, Gwyneth said, "Mr. Raith, we were just now contemplating an amiable walk on this very fine afternoon and wondered if such an excursion might appeal to you after your long journey?"

"An excellent suggestion," agreed Gavin, "just the thing to invigorate the constitution after the lethargy of travel."

In less than a moment, the party was suitably fitted for their country stroll, and they departed with suitably playful gaiety, Gavin centering himself between the two ladies and offering a gentleman's arm to each.

"I thought perhaps you might enjoy the coolness of the meadow," suggested Gwyneth.

"Oh yes!" eagerly added Isabella. "We could go across the meadow and down to the creek." She looked appealingly to Gavin as she explained, "Mr. Smithson, the gardener, reported seeing a most delightful baby deer drinking from the creek. Oh, do let's go see if it might still be there!"

"Let's do, indeed," confirmed Gavin. "I insist there is no more engaging sight in nature than a tiny fawn attempting to scamper on its spindly legs."

Engaged thus with good humor all, they proceeded with a lively, though not hurried, step. It was, indeed, a splendid day for a walk, what with the sunlight glancing brilliantly off the deep-green grasses and the wildflowers waving graciously in the soft breeze. The route of the walking party took them over a particularly grassy knoll that was skirted by a fragrant line of berry bushes that were, themselves, comfortably nestled in the midst of a rich variety of green vegetation that any proper deer would find profoundly succulent.

"There's the reason for your deer sightings," remarked Gavin. "I shouldn't be surprised if we spot a whole herd of the creatures somewhere nearby."

Pointing to the berries, Isabella asked, "Gwyny, do you think we might have some berries for our walk?"

"They do look freshly ripe," answered Gwyneth. "Mr. Raith?"

"Fresh berries it shall be," replied Gavin.

Each in the party took a separate bush. Gavin, looking more bemused than industrious, attacked the largest of the bushes while Gwyneth and Isabella more daintily approached smaller bushes on either side of Gavin. They worked quickly with much laughter and shouts of discovery, as the berries were plentiful. Suddenly, Isabella, reaching incautiously into a bush stealthily guarded by a barbed vine, cried out sharply in pain and just as suddenly withdrew her hand from the bush. Gavin, hurrying with genuine concern, hastened to her side to investigate what could be the matter.

"It's my finger," said Isabella, holding forth her finger to show Gavin.

A droplet of blood had gathered to the surface where evidently she had pricked her delicate skin. In his most courtly manner, Gavin took her hand in his, examined the injury with courteous concern, and then, leaning forward ever so slowly, ever so gently, kissed the tiny droplet away.

As Gavin unfolded from his gallant bow, a delightfully flustered Isabella, beaming her brightest, blushing smile, could only manage to say, "*Gracias, señor.*"

"At your service, m'lady," replied Gavin with an acknowledging nod of his head.

As Gwyneth arrived to peer intently at the wounded hand still held by Gavin, she asked anxiously, "Is it serious?"

In a fine parody of sobriety, Gavin replied, "I have ascertained that the injury is not excessive. It is my opinion that it may be best treated by an application of fresh air and the ointment of good company."

Amidst the shared laughter of Gavin's jest and satisfied that all was well, Gwyneth hurried back to retrieve the small satchel of berries that she had dropped when she was startled by Isabella's cry. As she did so, Gavin addressed Isabella in a discreetly hushed tone. "My dear Isabella, if you have any wish of my service, *any wish*," he emphasized, "you have but to indicate your desire, and I shall address it."

Isabella flushed at this exceptional attention that seemed to be of far greater measure than her minor injury merited. Suddenly awkward and uncertain of what reply would be deemed suitable or even expected, Isabella offered a noncommittal smile and then turned sprightly to wave to Gwyneth.

The remainder of the excursion was congenial and unremarkable except that the party returned in good appetite for the tea and cakes that would appear as a refreshment later in the mid-afternoon. Meanwhile,

Gavin took his leave to look for Cedric in the study where he, no doubt, would be examining some dreary document or ledger. Gwyneth and Isabella, in their turn, went to the large sitting room where they hoped to find Ariana. As they entered the sitting room, Lady Sylvia appeared to be consoling Ariana, who was looking dejected.

"It was only a misunderstanding," Lady Sylvia was saying to Ariana.

Gwyneth and Isabella, hearing the comment, paused at a short distance away that they might not intrude on a private matter. They, nonetheless, turned their questioning looks to Ariana, upon whom they depended for all matters needing resolution.

"Mr. Stacey had heard certain details of the fiasco with Mrs. Crandesol," explained Ariana, "and came to express his concern, which, it seems, has evolved into his unreserved disappointment in myself."

"Now, Ariana," scolded Lady Sylvia, "you know that is not so. I believe he now understands the situation and is content with our explanation. You must not let words unleashed in anger cause anxiety where none is warranted."

"Indeed," said Ariana without enthusiasm. "I know you to be correct, and I have no doubt that I shall return to good humor soon enough."

"Perhaps, then," said Lady Sylvia, speaking in her most matter-of-fact tone, "perhaps the best remedy I can offer you at this moment is to leave you in the care of Gwyneth and Isabella here, whose spirits appear to be considerably higher than either yours or mine."

"Thank you, Lady Sylvia," said Ariana contritely. "I am most appreciative of your support, and I truly shall strive to rally my spirit."

As Lady Sylvia departed, Gwyneth peered intently at her sister.

"Oh, Ari," she began, "tell me what I may do for you. I have never seen you so exceedingly distressed!"

For reply, Ariana could only issue the short, humorless laugh that is discharged when an untenable duress is relinquished.

"Am I so far gone then?" she asked, in an attempt to sound resolute.

"No," said Gwyneth, hastening to deny what was clear to her eyes. "No, you are not so far gone as all that. I only meant—"

"Yes, I know what you meant," assured Ariana. "Dear Gwyny, I know that you shall always do what I need you to do or be what I need you to be." She smiled encouragingly to Gwyneth and then looked to Isabella. "And you too, dear Isabella, you are a true friend. I cannot long be moping when there are two such people as you to cheer me up."

Straightening herself then and taking a deep breath, she said, "There, now. You must straightway tell me of your day and of those delights that have transpired to make you in such a rush to find me. And," she added with a good imitation of excellent humor, "do not say it is the anticipation of tea and cakes that makes you so radiant. That I shall not abide."

"No, not tea and cakes," said Gwyneth, becoming slightly mischievous, "but perhaps it was a delicious matter of a different sort."

"Gwyneth! Please, do not tease," pleaded Isabella, trying to repress a delighted smile that was quickening to a blush. "It certainly was not delicious!"

"I don't think Mr. Raith would agree with you there," said Gwyneth, with a hint of teasing incredulity. "He rather seemed to relish the little sip he imbibed from your very hand!"

"What's this?" asked Ariana with exaggerated interest, eager to accept the offered levity.

"I pricked my finger," declared Isabella, by way of protest and explanation at the same time, "and Mr. Raith was kind enough to attend to my injury."

"By kissing her finger," said Gwyneth in a lingering tone that suggested there was more to be said.

"It was bleeding!" protested Isabella to Ariana.

"I suppose," replied Ariana with mock reasoning, "there was no opportunity to blot it."

"Blot it?" objected Gwyneth. "Oh, Ari! How unromantic!"

"Ah," said Ariana in feigned enlightenment, "then it was to be heroic that Mr. Raith acted thus for Isabella."

"It was not heroic. It was not romantic," declared Isabella unconvincingly. "He was just being kind."

"Kind indeed," said Ariana.

"Indeed," said Gwyneth.

Chapter 11

In polite society, it is always understood that tea is a synonym for armistice. It is a time for reflection and rehabilitation. Umbrage is forbidden, and the only consideration permitted to rivals and adversaries is tolerance.

Accordingly, tea was served with no evidence of discord among the parties. With appropriate civility and decorum, Lady Sylvia and Ariana greeted Mr. Stacey and Mr. Raith, who arrived just moments after Gwyneth and Isabella, who were accompanied by Carlton Garrick. Mr. Stacey was all politeness as he addressed himself to Lady Sylvia, while Mr. Raith chose to cast a broad smile in the general direction of Gwyneth and Isabella, his eyes, though, being more selective in their particular attention to Isabella.

When everyone was settled with a cup of tea, Lady Sylvia directed the conversation toward the more or less neutral topic of Carlton's paintings.

"Mr. Garrick was just telling us about his latest sketches," said Lady Sylvia. "He has had a most marvelous idea that would merit notice even without our project at Southjoy Mission."

"You are far too kind," protested Carlton.

"Nonsense," replied Lady Sylvia, "and you know I do not support false modesty."

"I should like to hear what you plan," remarked Cedric, casually but not without a note of caution in his tone, the thought of another stratagem evolving without his prior approval leaving him ill at ease.

"The concept is simple enough," began Carlton. "I wanted to do more than to depict the physical appearance of Southjoy Mission or even its renovation. I wanted to capture its spirit. But my first attempts were rooted in the prejudicial diatribes, the distorted rumors, the fear and apprehensions that have haunted Southjoy Mission for as long as anyone can remember. I freely admit they were all I knew of Southjoy Mission outside of its physical appearance. As a result," said Carlton, smiling gratefully now toward Ariana, "my first sketches were dark and brooding, as Ariana rightly described them."

"And have you found a way past those perceptions?" asked Cedric, without looking toward Ariana.

"Yes, thanks to Gwyneth," he replied but recanted quickly to say, "Well, thanks first to Ariana and then to Gwyneth. You see," he said, settling himself more comfortably into his chair, "Ariana asked me to do a sketch of Gwyneth sitting in the atrium." He looked toward Cedric as he explained, "To encourage me to see Southjoy Mission in a different light. It changes the context, you understand." He smiled somewhat self-consciously as he said, "I was delighted by the opportunity and began that same day. Over the next few days, I tried a variety of poses in several different locations."

He acquired a more studious concentration as he continued, "During one of those sittings, I must have been a bit distracted, for Gwyneth remarked upon it and inquired as to why that might be. My response, unreserved as it always is with Gwyneth, was to confess how I felt that, inwardly, I had not yet discovered the poetic soul of the mansion. Instantly, as I but laid this confession before her, she turned to me that most expressive face of hers and said with considerable excitement that there was a book in the library that I must see. She was most insistent on this point."

As Carlton paused to smile at Gwyneth, Gavin was suddenly seized by an insuppressible laugh as though he were suddenly enlightened to a secret humor. "Not *the* book," he declared in mock concern, "not the infamous history!"

Cedric, looking mildly puzzled, spoke to Gavin, "You know what book they are speaking of?"

"I believe I do," replied Gavin, "if I am not mistaken?" he asked, looking toward Ariana.

"It is, indeed, the book from the library," said Ariana with an acknowledging tilt of her head, there being only one book bearing their mutual acquaintanceship in the library.

"And would someone care to enlighten me?" asked Cedric.

"And me," added Lady Sylvia.

"There is a small, nondescript book in the library," said Ariana by way of explanation, "entitled, *The True and Right History of the Heresy of Edmund Plagyts*."

"Ah, yes, that book," said Cedric with a bemused glance toward Ariana. "I recall now, Gavin, you related to me the saga of your adventure in the library concerning that book during our first visit here."

"That book," said Ariana stiffly, "relates an unfortunate incident of inquisition that took place here at Southjoy Mission and may account for its unsavory reputation."

"I see, yes," said Lady Sylvia. "I understand the relevance now."

"And it is that understanding," said Carlton, continuing with the discussion of his project, "that has inspired me. You see," he now spoke excitedly, "there is a story here that touches on human issues of suffering and compassion, and therein lies the very birth of art or, at least, the nourishment of the artist. I shall depict the history of Southjoy Mission as the sufferance of abuse while portraying its renovation as a transcendence to glory."

The finality and conviction of this statement were unmistakable and were greeted with much enthusiasm by the ladies and with sober approval by Mr. Stacey, seconded by Mr. Raith.

As Gwyneth and Isabella hovered about Carlton in congratulatory excitement, Gavin took the opportunity to approach Ariana.

"Miss Ariana," he spoke formally in a lowered voice, "my sincere apology if I have embarrassed you in any way in front of Mr. Stacey. If you would but give me the opportunity to correct that perception and any other misunderstanding," he added parenthetically, "that might have occurred between us, I would be honored to do so. As you no doubt have seen, I have some degree of influence with Mr. Stacey, even in these small matters. Should you wish it, I would speak to him on your behalf."

Ariana looked at him intently, as one peers into the distance in an earnest attempt to discover the identity of the blurry figure that approaches from far away.

"That is most generous of you, Mr. Raith," she said cautiously. Ariana hesitated before responding further.

There was something spoken in his manner that was not spoken in his words. He leaned—nay, loomed—over her as he now stood beside the seated Ariana. He looked down onto her as a master looks down upon a servant. She turned her head away from him and then looked aimlessly into an empty space in the room.

"I thank you for your good intentions," said Ariana. "They are, indeed, kind, but I think my constitution will survive even this censure from Mr. Stacey."

As she turned to look toward Cedric, Gavin stooped beside her, partially kneeling, placing his hand upon hers.

"I am persuaded we could be friends," he said in a hushed, confidential tone. "Good friends."

Ariana stiffened slightly, looking quickly from Gavin to Isabella and back to Gavin again. She withdrew her hand sharply just as Gwyneth asked from across the room, "You two are not still arguing about that book, are you?"

"No," protested Ariana, feeling greatly ill at ease.

"No, indeed," said Gavin, rising smoothly. "We have finished with arguing, I believe."

He offered a parting smile to Ariana as he moved to join Cedric and Lady Sylvia.

When the obligations of tea had been satisfied, the parties separated to pursue their respective activities. Cedric, accompanied by Gavin, took advantage of the fine early evening to inspect the grounds and some of the outlying buildings. As they walked, Cedric principally confined his remarks to the prospects of the property, to which Gavin replied with suitable appreciation. He alluded to Lady Sylvia only once and to Ariana not at all. For their parts, Lady Sylvia and

Ariana, anxious now to see Carlton's progress, went to review the sketches he had made earlier that morning. Ariana was relieved that this occupation spared her any further discourse concerning either Mr. Stacey or Mr. Raith. Gwyneth, Isabella, and Carlton, who were the first to adjourn from the tearoom, removed themselves by prearrangement to the atrium garden, now a favorite among the places of retreat at Southjoy Mission. There, at Gwyneth's suggestion, Carlton was undertaking to sketch Isabella sitting highlighted by the pre-twilight sun amidst dramatic lengthening shadows.

The remainder of the day progressed in the most natural of courses, and the party did not reassemble until just before dinner. As Gavin joined the assembly, he particularly sought the attention of Ariana, who particularly avoided his attention by turning away as though she had not seen the inquiring smile he cast in her direction. The scowl that suddenly clouded Mr. Raith's face showed his displeasure, which was further evidenced by the curt greeting he offered to Cedric. The latter gentleman being distracted by a comment from Lady Sylvia allowed the gruffness of Gavin's manner to go unnoticed except as it suggested that Mr. Raith might be predisposed to fatigue after the strenuous walk they had conducted earlier that evening.

Mr. Raith, however, was not so easily to be dissuaded and made yet a second overture to Ariana, who, though polite, was otherwise unreceptive. Mr. Stacey, noting their close proximity at that moment, surmised a degree of familiarity that occasioned him a mild sense of surprise. It was not disapproval, precisely, but, perhaps, only an inclination to caution that quickened his senses. The thought certainly had already occurred to him that an unscrupulous person might try to take advantage of her position with Lady Sylvia to better herself, and if not through himself, then through his friend. However, he dismissed this thought at once as Ariana took two decisive steps away from Gavin. Oddly, this observation of strain between Ariana and Gavin seemed to lessen his own.

Mr. Raith, himself, did not seem to suffer any ill effect from the incident. Indeed, exhibiting no evidence of rebuff, he quickly regained his composure, applied his most appealing smile to his face, and straightway offered congenial greetings to Isabella and Gwyneth. This redistribution of attention and courtesy continued into dinner. As Mr. Raith was seated between Ariana and Isabella, Mr. Raith's predilection to Isabella was accomplished at the neglect of Ariana. In consequence, Mr. Stacey, who was, of course, seated at the head of the table, was left to converse in idle conversation with Ariana, on his right, and Gwyneth, on his left. The one being considered unworthy and the other of no significance, this alignment of neighboring diners imparted a certain taxing annoyance to Mr. Stacey's courteous demeanor. From time to time, Cedric found himself frowning at Gavin. Whether this was due to his own awkward circumstance or to the fact that Isabella was too young to be receiving so much admiring attention from Mr. Raith, or merely the consequence of his own lack of witty, worldly, or otherwise stimulating remarks to Ariana and her sister, was uncertain.

The atmosphere in the sitting room after dinner was congenial and not in the least strained by conflict or innuendo. Lady Sylvia was recounting a charming memory of Sir Waverly to Cedric, who found it suitably engaging, while Gavin was serving as an inattentive audience to Gwyneth's performance of a piano concerto for which Carlton was delighted to serve as page turner. Isabella had approached Ariana with an apparent desire to talk in some degree of confidence, and they were now taking a turn about the room while speaking softly.

"Ariana," began Isabella, "is he, Mr. Raith that is, very much a gentleman?"

"Mr. Raith?" replied Ariana cautiously, matching Isabella's tone. "He is respected by Mr. Stacey. That is certain, I think." Suddenly thinking of what Gavin might be saying about herself, she ventured, "Why do you ask? Have you heard something about him or one of us?"

"No, nothing like that," said Isabella. "It is just something he said to me. I am not sure what it means."

As they paced themselves slowly in a casual progression without particular aim, Ariana noted how Isabella was nervously toying with the small ribbon on the handle of the fan she held closed in her hand. Such a mannerism was not usual for her, and alerted by this observation, Ariana asked with concern, "Isabella, whatever could it be?"

"At dinner this evening," said Isabella, "at first," she clarified, "he seemed to be teasing me about pricking my finger when we were gathering berries. He said something amusing. I don't remember now exactly what it was…something about how I was planning to bite the berries, and it was they who bit me. Something like that. Anyway, we laughed. But then, quite suddenly, he was very serious, and he reminded me of what he had said at that time, something, I had to confess, I had not thought about until he reminded me. He said to me that if I would wish for anything, it would be his wish to address it." She paused momentarily as they stopped to admire a small porcelain figurine. "I thought he might still be teasing me, and so I laughed a little again. But then he repeated it, and he seemed very earnest about it."

"And you want to know what he could mean by such an earnest offer," suggested Ariana.

"No, not that exactly," said Isabella. "It was what he said later."

They smiled pleasantly toward Gwyneth, who had finished playing and was being encouraged by Carlton to play more. As Gwyneth began a second piece, Ariana and Isabella began a second turn about the room.

"Later," continued Isabella, "I think you were speaking with Mr. Stacey just then, he became serious again. He said he admired me, and he said he could see that I admired him but that perhaps I needed something more to be convinced altogether of his admiration. Then he put his hand on mine and said if, perhaps, I would arrange to meet him alone later tonight, I would be convinced beyond all doubt."

"Isabella!" declared Ariana in whispered astonishment. Frantically looking then to the others to be sure no one had noticed the changed intensity of their discourse, she began, "Surely he didn't," but stopped as quickly as begun, such was the degree to which her thoughts were confounded, not only by what Isabella had just confided, but also by the memory of this same Mr. Raith placing his hand on her, Ariana's, own hand just moments prior to turning his attention to Isabella.

"I didn't know what to say," said Isabella, rushing on, "so I said nothing. I think I was afraid a little that I would say something wrong, so I said nothing." She paused then, glancing at Ariana for emphasis. "He just waited," she said simply, as though marveling at the fact, "and when I did not speak, he just smiled at me." Again changing her tone to one of caution, she continued, "Then he said he knew that I would think about it, and he would wait for word from me." Then, looking with all the intensity of innocence enhanced by a newly awakened desire, she pleaded, "Oh, Ariana, you must tell me! Did I do wrong? Should I have answered him at once?" Then, as with a sudden thought and the alarm to accompany it, she asked, "Do you think I have offended him? Oh, Ariana, I would not want to cause more trouble with Mr. Stacey."

Ariana, discreetly inhaling deeply to steady herself, placed her hand reassuringly on Isabella's arm.

"Of Mr. Stacey," she said with the rational calm of someone who most wanted to be irrational at just that moment, "you need harbor no concern. And you were right to say nothing to Mr. Raith!" she whispered emphatically. "And indeed, for now say nothing more to Mr. Raith." She paused as she looked pleasantly about the room and then said, "We need to talk more, but we cannot do it here. Indeed," she emphasized with a further note of resolve, "you and I and Gwyneth have much to discuss concerning the adventures of Mr. Raith."

The sudden look of surprise on Isabella's face was sufficient testimony that she understood, if not the detail, then the import of Ariana's statement.

For the remainder of the social evening, Ariana appeared to be distracted, while Isabella seemed to be nervous, even anxious, about something. It was generally assumed that Ariana was still brooding about Mr. Stacey's censure, and Lady Sylvia even made a point of declaring her support for Ariana by way of dispelling any concern she might yet be nursing on that account. Isabella's unsettled nerves were generally dismissed as the consequence of an overly strenuous day for someone so young. Mr. Raith, though, chose to see them as evidence that she was contemplating an advantageous response to his proposition. It was, therefore, to no one's surprise that both Ariana and Isabella excused themselves to retire early. Gwyneth chose to join them, of course, while Lady Sylvia announced that she had a few minor matters to attend to, leaving the gentlemen to retire at their leisure.

Gwyneth, ever alert to her sister's moods, hurried after Ariana and Isabella.

"I do believe you two have been plotting some intrigue," she said keenly. "Am I to know what it is? You have been whispering a great deal."

As the ensemble reconvened in Ariana's bedroom, Ariana replied, "Intrigue it shall be." When the door was securely closed, she continued rather factually and summarily, "Dear Isabella has received from Mr. Raith a rather improper proposal bearing more than a hint of intimacy in its suggestion."

Gwyneth hesitated as though she had misheard what was said. "Isabella?" she asked and then stopped in disbelief of its possibility. "No!" she declared in the firmness of her disbelief. "I had rather imagined some careless remark had been made or overheard, something frightfully rude or even some further discord incited by Mr. Stacey, but, Ariana, consider! The accusation you place against the conduct of Mr. Raith is outrageous!"

"Outrageous, yes, and worse," continued Ariana, dramatically highlighting her words with darker tones. "I also do not believe his proposal to be honorable in any respect, for I, too," she said now in a tone of some little repulsion, "I, too, have received from Mr. Raith declarations of such similar address as to cast doubt on his intentions toward either of us."

"Ariana," gasped Gwyneth, "you cannot mean..." Then she fell silent as her mind whirled in utter amazement.

Isabella, grasping both hands to her flushed face, could only stare at Ariana as disbelief struggled against dismay. Doubts assailed her thoughts, denials wailed, "Foul injury!," and even the searing flames of jealousy filled her eyes with recrimination, all looming and receding in rapid succession. Then, patiently, as it must in the unyielding clasp of true friendship, the cacophony of outrage subsided and was swept away by a breathless, demanding clamor for a just resolution.

"Isabella," said Ariana softly, "I am truly sorry if this is hurtful to you. In the end, I know that you shall rally, as, indeed, my own experience has shown by example."

Isabella looked sharply away, still struggling with her thoughts, still wishing it could be otherwise. Then, turning slowly back to Ariana, she replied in a subdued voice, strained only a little by a remnant dismay, "Thank you, but no," she resolved, "I shall not be so easily injured when I have such friends as you and Gwyneth." She paused, smiling faintly, then added with a hint of longing reluctance, "It was pleasing, though, to be singled out for special attention." Then as disappointment dissipated in the chagrin of understanding, she concluded, "But I see now that it was attention only and not affection."

Gwyneth smiled softly at Isabella. "Sages have struggled for centuries to say in their elegant phrases what you have said so simply, and they have not half the clarity."

After a few moments of soft conversation to ensure that each and all were well apprised of the circumstances of Mr. Raith's intentions and suitably armored against them, Ariana turned to the immediate issue. "How, then, are we to respond to Mr. Raith's false overtures?"

"We must confront him and demand his apology," declared Isabella, now feisty and incensed with the indignity of offense.

"Yes," said Ariana, "were he an honorable person, wholly honorable," she qualified, "it would be sufficient to enlighten him as to the offense, and he would recant it at once. But I rather think Mr. Raith would derive a certain enjoyment from a confrontation. He would only laugh at us and declare us to be silly girls and accuse us of romantic imaginings designed to enliven our dreary lives, and I fear Mr. Stacey would believe him."

"Surely not Mr. Stacey," said Isabella hopefully.

"Would not Lady Sylvia persuade him that you, at least, are not so susceptible to flights of fancy?" asked Gwyneth.

"Mr. Stacey," said Ariana with a note of resignation, "has already accused me of abusing my position with Lady Sylvia to insinuate myself into a situation beyond my station. He is unlikely to be persuaded otherwise if his friend accuses me likewise."

"He can't truly believe such a thing of you, of all people," said Isabella, now rallying to Ariana's support.

"Unfortunately, he was most serious," replied Ariana.

"With so much in opposition, what then can be done?" asked Gwyneth.

"If they are not to believe us," said Ariana rather factually, "then we must let them see for themselves."

"'They' being Lady Sylvia and Mr. Stacey," clarified Gwyneth.

"Precisely," said Ariana, already deep in thought.

"And Mr. Raith?"

"We must contrive for Mr. Raith to be the Mr. Raith that we know him to be."

Gwyneth, looking slyly at Ariana, asked, "Ariana, whatever are you thinking?"

"I am thinking that Mr. Raith is waiting for a response from Isabella, so"—Ariana smiled—"we shall give him one."

Chapter 12

The note had been slipped under the door of his bedroom. Gavin's spirit bounded at the sight of it, for it could only have come from one party. He had chuckled to himself when Isabella had retired without so much as looking at him. Throughout the evening, she had seemed nervous and had avoided his attentions. He had concluded from her conduct that she was, in the end, just a frightened child not sufficiently advanced for an amorous adventure. But not so, for here was a reply that showed how slyly she was prepared for him.

The note said only, "east end guest room at midnight," but it was enough.

Renovations of the eastern quarters had not yet begun, so the rooms there were currently unoccupied. Any assignation there would be undisturbed. Clever indeed.

Waiting for the appointed hour afforded him much opportunity for impatience. At regular intervals, he tested his bedroom door to assure himself that it could be opened without creaking or producing other sounds that might raise an alarm among the occupants of the neighboring rooms. As each of the multitude of household sounds drifted into silence, he listened intently until, as midnight approached, Southjoy Mission nestled into a calm, restful, soundless peace.

Stealthily, then, Gavin opened his door and slipped into the hallway. He paused, listening momentarily for signs of disturbance. Detecting none, he closed the door, listened again, and then quietly, stepping with purpose as warily as any thief in the night, he moved down the hallway, turning at the landing to proceed to the far end of the eastern corridor. There, he found the door to the end room slightly ajar. Pushing gently, the door opened freely.

From their vantage point in the corner room by the landing, where the conspirators had watched as Gavin slowly made his way down the hallway, Ariana nodded to Carlton, who had allied himself with the conspiracy as a willing recruit. Decisive timing was imperative for their plan. Too much delay and Gavin would sense something awry and would vacate the room. Acknowledging his readiness to Ariana, Carlton departed to find Mr. Stacey the instant Gavin disappeared into the fated chamber.

The room appointed for the assignation was brightly illuminated by moonlight streaming through an uncovered window. Rapidly surveying the room, Gavin readily perceived that linen had been quickly, but adequately, laid over the bed and turned back invitingly. Beside the bed stood a small table on which a bottle of sherry rested, along with two partially filled glasses at its side. A note lay upon the pillow.

"Make yourself ready," it said. "Clink the glasses twice. Close your eyes and wait." The last phrase was underlined twice, doubling its delight. "This time," the note concluded, "a sweeter nectar!"

Gavin inhaled deeply with even greater delight, for the allusion could only be to the adventure of the succulent berries and of the tiny droplet he had kissed from Isabella's finger.

Noting, then, a lady's night wrap casually draped over a chair in the corner of the room, Gavin quickly glanced about the room looking for other signs of her presence. Finding none, he smiled with growing anticipation, for he must have surprised her, causing her to go into hiding with some haste. Inspired by a charmingly romantic humor, he went to the garment and carefully laid Isabella's note upon it, an invitation in reply to an invitation. Never had a conquest been so effortless, and how appropriate the signal to his amour — to raise the glasses fragrant with wine and to clink them in toast of the delight to follow. As he smiled at his good fortune, a momentary confusion intercepted his reverie, causing him to hesitate for the briefest of instants, but enough to disturb his train of thought. The preparations seemed too sophisticated, too calmly deliberate, not impetuous and impatient, as he would expect of young Isabella. Everything here seemed controlled and confident, as might be expected of Ariana. But all this romantic fantasy from Ariana the Sensible? He marveled at the possibility. He looked again at the linen invitingly turned back, the sherry already poured. It was all too delicious! And what matter if it proved to be Ariana or Isabella? The uncertainty but added to his anticipation.

A soft, insistent knocking jarred Cedric's bed chamber door. Having just nicely slipped into a deep sleep, Cedric was not pleased to be awakened so soon. Scowling as he opened the door, he was surprised to find an anxious Carlton waiting for him.

"I think you'd better come—quickly!" urged Carlton before Cedric could speak. "There's a noise coming from the far end of the east corridor."

"At this hour?" question Cedric, not fully awake.

"Precisely," emphasized Carlton. "I thought to investigate it myself, but then I thought it would be better to get you first, not knowing what the cause might be."

"Yes, of course," replied Cedric. Rapidly gathering his wits, he considered what could possibly account for a disturbance at this late hour but found no ready explanation that was sufficiently plausible.

"I suppose it could be a squirrel or a raccoon," suggested Carlton.

Cedric dismissed the idea, for although the renovation of the east corridor would not commence for some time yet, it was not dilapidated or in disrepair.

"A burglar, then?"

"A possibility, but there isn't anything of value in those quarters to entice a burglar." Cedric shook his head. There was nothing for it. As titular head of the family, he must investigate it.

Now fully awake and ready for action, Cedric dispatched Carlton to rouse Gavin so as to increase their number for the purposes of both safety and expedience. He himself took the opportunity to fetch one of Sir Waverly's hunting rifles as a precaution against the extraordinary event that an intervention of force might be required.

Carlton's return was greeted by a puzzled frown on Cedric's face when the former returned unaccompanied by Gavin.

"You couldn't wake him?" asked Cedric, seeking clarification.

"No, he wasn't there to be woken," replied Carlton. "I opened the door and found the room empty."

Carlton benignly chose not to mention the note he found lying on the table in the room and which he had forthrightly tucked into his pocket. Later, at a suitably opportune time, he would discreetly return the conspiratorial piece of paper to Ariana.

Cedric, endeavoring to understand the peculiar absence of his friend and finding no ready explanation, chose the only course open to him.

"No matter," he said, stepping briskly, "let us be off."

As they approached the end of the corridor, the light from the lantern carried by Carlton revealed that the end door that ought ordinarily to be closed was slightly ajar. As Cedric pushed softly to open the door slowly, a voice from within the room whispered somewhat musically, "Come in, my sweet. How long I have waited for you!"

Cedric, taken aback in utter amazement at what he had just heard, thrust the door open sharply, stepping into the room as he did so, followed closely by Carlton.

Surprise mired the three gentlemen into a motionless frieze. It could have been a masterwork, "Don Juan Discovered." At the open door, the irate lord of the manor stands with musket in hand, while slightly behind the protective shoulder of his master is the faithful servant holding forth in one hand a glaring lantern that shed streams of light upon the chagrined image of the discovered Don.

The sudden burst of voices emanating from the small room echoed throughout the corridor, and in short order, the entire household was awake and in motion, all convening at the fateful room to witness the bizarre affair unfolding there. Lady Sylvia and Ariana arrived almost together with Gwyneth and Isabella close behind.

As they gathered in the room, Gavin heaved rather than spoke an exasperated, "Oh, good lord."

Cedric, looking toward the new arrivals and holding his arms out as though to collect the swelling crowd together, said with deliberate calm, "Ladies, this might not be a proper place for your presence."

"It seems to me," replied Lady Sylvia without hesitation, "this is not a proper place for anyone. What is the meaning of this," she asked, addressing Cedric, and added with some degree of irritation, "and this unruly commotion at this late hour?"

Cedric, beset with mixed sensibilities and despite his good imagination, appeared uncertain as to how to reply.

Choosing the most neutral of tones affordable to the moment, he said objectively, "What was intended, I have not fully ascertained. Whatever that may have been, however, it appears that it has not yet transpired."

"I am much relieved to hear it," said Lady Sylvia whose vivid note of reprimand amplified the intent of her words.

At just that moment, Isabella, who had been glancing about the room with considerable interest, suddenly declared, "That," pointing at the cloak draped over a chair, "that belongs to me!"

With unhesitating and determined steps, she marched to the chair. Seeing the note as she did so, she carefully tucked it into the folds of her garment even as she seized the garment and held it aloft for all to see.

Turning sharply, she pointed the garment accusingly at Gavin, whose regard heretofore she had avoided.

"You were in my room?" she asked, her voice ringing with indignity.

Gavin stared at the evidence as though seeing it for the first time. "No," he cried hastily, "that's not mine."

Briefly bemused by Gavin's peculiar response, Cedric commented lightly, "I should hope it isn't."

The levity, however brief, was sufficient to restore some small measure of wit to Gavin's thoughts.

"You know what I mean," he appealed to Cedric. "I have never seen that garment before, and I don't know how it got here." As he spoke, his face was already growing dark as his mind raced ahead with his next thoughts. "But I can tell you one thing," he said with angry certainty, "I have been ill used!"

"You mean to say," asked Lady Sylvia, whose powers of observation and deduction were not the least impaired by age or circumstance, "that because you have been thwarted in your attempt to seduce a member of this household, you have been abused?"

Gavin, stung by such direct accusation, turned first one way then the other, a clammy sweat beginning to cling to his hands. Suddenly, he pointed at Ariana. "You!" he declared as though he had just comprehended a mystery. "It was you," he accused.

Before other response could be hurled into the fray, Cedric, whose powers of observation were second to none, interjected a resonant and conclusive, "Enough," as though making a tiresome judgment. "Next you will be accusing me." He smiled humorlessly at Gavin, conveying in his look that he had surmised as much as he cared to know about the present affair and wished to hear nothing more. "Evidently," he continued, "you have all had your amusements here, to which I have not been a party, and for my part, I wish that it remain so. Everything that has or was about to occur here is at an end. For now," he said with enforced equanimity, "everyone go back to your rooms, and take what sleep as may yet be had."

The staff that had formed a small crowd outside the room dispersed quickly, while those inside vacated the room only with considerable reluctance.

Cedric, ushering the others out of the room, was the last, but Gavin, to leave.

Turning back as he departed, Cedric said somewhat caustically, "You and I will talk more tomorrow."

Gavin, dark with frustration, acknowledged Cedric with a tired, resigned wave of his hand. Inwardly, though, he was already seething with schemes of vengeance on Miss Ariana Atwood, on whom his displeasure had sharply focused into a finely honed wrath.

Chapter 13

The morning arrived in relative calm. Gavin did not present himself for breakfast and delayed making his appearance until he knew Cedric would be in the study. He found him there, sitting rigidly in the chair behind the great desk, sipping a cup of tea, and looking aimlessly out the window.

Speaking without looking away from the window, Cedric said rather simply, "Let us have it, then—your account of the bizarre events of last night."

Having received no invitation to sit, Gavin hesitated and then adopted an attitude of speaking frankly with a friend. He slumped into the nearest chair, inhaled deeply, and then quickly sat forward on the edge of the seat.

"It was that bitter, conniving, scheming Ariana!" he said heatedly.

He had thought, belatedly, to bring the notes he had received to bolster his claim, but when he had gone in search of them, neither was to be found. Seeing ever more clearly the trap laid for him, he resolved then to be the accuser, to be the victim of the heartless Ariana. After all, it had been a successful defense in other scandals and would, perhaps, work yet again.

Without stirring or altering his gaze, Cedric chose to reply to Gavin's declaration with the studied calm of neutrality.

"I would prefer that you report only the events as they pertain to last night's affair and that you not address yourself to any characterization of Miss Atwood, for," he added almost whimsically, "I will otherwise suspect that she is not so sinister as you suggest."

Calmly, then, he permitted Gavin to tell his carefully crafted defense, to explain how it was Ariana who led him on, how he merely joined in with a bit of flirtation, how Ariana must have misunderstood, how it was she who had intimated that she might be receptive to a rendezvous.

He concluded with, "Good heavens! What was I to think?" Speaking frankly then in his best man-to-man tone, he allowed, "After all, she is attractive, as country girls measure, and I am encumbered by no attachment, as you know."

He paused to see if Cedric would, at least, acknowledge that much.

Seeing Cedric's thoughtful pose unaltered, Gavin finished with, "That, upon my honor, is all there was to it, at least as to the cause of last night's fiasco. The rest you know."

Speaking, then, without looking in Gavin's direction, Cedric said firmly, "I have given you this opportunity to describe the events of last night without interruption in respect of our friendship. I am persuaded that what you considered harmless flirtation could well have been misinterpreted by the rustic sensibilities of Miss Atwood. I might have expected you to be more aware of your own, shall we say, charm, but I cannot fault you for any lapse owing to Miss Atwood's own judgment."

Cedric momentarily became very quiet. Then, with sudden verve, he whirled to face Gavin, his hand slapping hard upon the desk as he turned.

As Gavin flinched, Cedric's voice rang out in harsh indictment, "But I do find much fault and effrontery with the location of your seduction. This is the home of Lady Sylvia! And you would make it a brothel in her presence and mine?"

Pointing his finger sharply at Gavin, he added with much exasperation, "You may well believe I am much disappointed in you."

As he glared at Gavin, the latter tried to appear repentant. "Your conduct," declared Cedric, "wounds me with its abuse of our friendship and places me in a most compromising position."

"My dear Cedric," Gavin urgently pleaded, "for dearer to me are you than any brother could be. We have endured trials and circumstances that have forged an uncommon bond between us. Surely you must know, had I thought for a moment there was any possibility of discovery, I should have aborted the adventure on the instant." Speaking in tones of self-reproach, he added, "It must be dashed embarrassing for you, I know, as it is for me. You have my word that I would not for a moment knowingly act in any manner that would compromise you or our friendship. I would even now make amends a thousand times over if I could, but in this circumstance, I can offer only this: You know me. You know that I have always spoken to you in unreserved loyalty. Say but the word, and I shall depart at once."

As the two men fell silent, Cedric turned again to regain his studied posture of gazing through a window in aimless distraction. Calmly, then, he said, "I am persuaded to weigh this affair on the fair balance of friendship that we have sustained these many years. Let us put this matter behind us, conclude it without reservation, as friends must do, and therein, consider all between us as settled."

Still not quite ready to look at his friend, he said quietly, "I will speak to Lady Sylvia to conclude the matter."

"And, no doubt, his statements were ambiguous as to their intent."

Lady Sylvia looked appropriately judicial as she, nonetheless, peered with a certain partiality of satisfaction across the table at Ariana, who sat comfortably with only a slight remnant of defiance lightly layered upon her otherwise properly posed demeanor.

Lady Sylvia had greeted Ariana with, "I am sure you are eager to speak of the events of last night, just as I am certain that you are possessed of more knowledge of those events than could be deduced by a mere observer."

"You are quite correct in both assumptions," replied Ariana, who set forth at once to report the particulars of the occasion in a most forthright manner, sparing none of the details about Gavin's flirtation with both herself and Isabella. She was vigorously seconded in every detail by a still exhilarated Isabella. Lady Sylvia, appalled that her niece would be the object of any attempted seduction, let alone a nefarious one, tried to caution Isabella to temper her enthusiasm. But Isabella would not be deterred and spoke willingly and eagerly of her own role in the adventure.

"So the three of you concocted this affair to embarrass Mr. Raith."

"Not so much to embarrass him as to teach him a lesson in respecting women and the standards of decorum in good society."

"And Mr. Garrick, was he part of the conspiracy?"

"I'm afraid that was my contribution," said Gwyneth sheepishly. "I knew he would be sketching late."

"And you knew he would not refuse you," said Lady Sylvia, not waiting for a reply from Gwyneth, whose only response, therefore, was a modest blushing about her cheeks.

"I think I understand your motivation," she continued, "and though I cannot condone your method, I do, at least, understand it." Speaking, then, in a lighter tone, she added, "I understand your excitement too. It was a rather daring thing to do, after all."

"Yes, it was!" beamed Isabella, casting aside all restraint. "It was thrilling beyond anything I have ever known, and if he was embarrassed, then good! He deserved every moment of it," she declared triumphantly.

"Thrilling, yes, of that I am sure, but I would caution you to exhibit less exhilaration lest you be found vindictive and wanting in charity yourself."

Properly chastised and contrite, Isabella acknowledged the propriety of Lady Sylvia's remark and instantly offered a properly obedient deference to her elders. She could not, however, properly subdue the incandescent delight that glowed in her eyes, nor prevent its reflection in perfect harmony with the properly averted smiles on the faces of Ariana and Gwyneth.

As Lady Sylvia properly suppressed the smile on her own face, she concluded by way of a show of reprimand with, "I think there could have been more acceptable forms of resolution had you confided in me before the affair rather than after it. I trust we shall not, in the future, witness a repeat of these circumstances."

"I think we shall all endeavor to derive as much benefit as possible from this affair," answered Ariana softly, and with complete sincerity.

"And to apply it unsparingly to our own standards of conduct," added Gwyneth, matching Ariana's sincerity. To all of which, Isabella, judiciously silent, nodded her sincere agreement as well.

"I am persuaded of the sincerity of your resolution," said Lady Sylvia, "and I trust that it shall be so."

Another concern suddenly worried Ariana.

"Is it necessary to reveal to Mr. Stacey all that we have told you? I am concerned that Mr. Stacey might react in anger should he learn of Mr. Raith's proposition to Isabella. For the same reason, I think it unlikely that Mr. Raith will divulge that situation to Mr. Stacey. He will, instead, blame me for everything." Ariana did not hesitate in drawing what would seem to be a necessary conclusion. "I think it might be wiser not to exacerbate the situation unnecessarily. I would prefer to spare Isabella the unjust calumny that might otherwise arise against her."

"Ariana, no," objected Isabella defiantly, looking desperately to Lady Sylvia for support, but Lady Sylvia was already acknowledging the sensibility of Ariana's understanding, for the thought of Cedric enraged was unsupportable.

"I fear Ariana is quite right. Cedric is a most capable person, but in this case, where the reputation of the family is involved, I fear Ariana's concern is more than justified. It is probable. We must be mindful that gossip travels quickly, even from loyal servants, and people often exercise more keenness to be unkind in their gossip than to be understanding. When the matter involves the reputation of a young girl, their delight in the cruelty of their prattle seems to invigorate its dissemination to an exaggerated degree. I believe we must also consider that when wrath erupts in someone as controlled as Cedric, its outcome may be quite unpredictable, even irrational."

It was a sobering thought that plunged the ensemble into a thoughtful silence that was, at length, broken by Gwyneth. Recalling at that moment an aphorism befitting the situation, she remarked, "Better disdain than sorrow."

There was a hint of resentment in her tone owing no doubt to the unfairness of the moment. She softened her tone at once, though, truer to her own spirit, to conclude with the promise, "For there shall yet be a morrow, wherein all answers follow."

Ariana nodded agreement, as did Lady Sylvia, although reluctantly.

"There is no other choice if we are to be prudent and sensible," said Ariana. "And Gwyneth is quite right," she added. "I would rather live with the disdain of others than the remorse of self, knowing that I could have prevented an injustice and did not."

Lady Sylvia looked upon Ariana with a mixture of sympathy and admiration.

"It will be an additional burden for you to bear."

Ariana, resigned to be, once again, the recipient of Mr. Stacey's ill opinion, nodded her understanding of this likelihood too. Indeed, she knew it to be a certainty, for even as she saw the rightness of her offer, she had sensed, felt intimately, a darkly tragic shadow beginning to draw over her spirit.

"I shall speak to Mr. Stacey," said Lady Sylvia, the amber tones of her own sadness layered densely upon her resolute decision.

Lady Sylvia chose to receive her nephew in her private quarters where the softer, more genteel surroundings might incline the interview to a more subdued and civil discourse.

"I do not believe it to be a mere coincidence," began Cedric, "that the name Miss Ariana Atwood is at the center of yet another unpleasantness."

"You surprise me, Cedric," interjected Lady Sylvia, "for it seems to me that the matter is rather more clearly centered on your friend, Mr. Raith, if I remember it correctly. I presume you have spoken to him and have inquired of his intentions in this most peculiar affair."

"His and Miss Atwood's, yes," replied Cedric with sufficient firmness to suggest the certainty of his position.

"Then you have spoken to Miss Atwood as well," said Lady Sylvia in a tone of satisfaction. "I am much relieved to hear it."

"No, not to Miss Atwood," said Mr. Stacey with but a hint of defensiveness in his tone. "Mr. Raith was most forthcoming concerning Miss Atwood's flirtations and freely admitted his own susceptibility to her charms. I am persuaded of his sincerity in this matter and that Miss Atwood has abused both her position and your trust."

"Then you would have her censured without defense?" There was a note of surprise in Lady Sylvia's question.

Responding to her tone, Mr. Stacey suggested, "It is a matter of honor, not of testimony, and in that respect, I think it is fortunate, for if were it a matter of testimony, I fear I should find Miss Atwood to be an unreliable witness."

"In that case," replied Lady Sylvia, "let me put your mind at ease regarding her testimony, for I have spoken to her, and also to Isabella, and I have concluded that there has been nothing in the conduct of Miss Atwood that I would endeavor to reprehend."

The countenance of Mr. Stacey began to exhibit its own dark testimony of frustration.

"It seems to me," continued Lady Sylvia so as to yield no quarter, "both parties have acknowledged that there was some degree of flirtation. To that extent, they are both at fault, if flirtation is now a fault and either is to be accused of wrongdoing."

"A tryst is no mere flirtation!" protested Cedric.

"Indeed it is not, but I am inclined to believe Miss Atwood that there was no intent on her part ever to consummate such a tryst. As we well know," she added with an air of stating the self-evident, "the same cannot be said of Mr. Raith."

Seizing on the last vestige of his argument, Cedric asserted, "But even so, intended or pretended, you must then admit that this whole affair was a deliberate attempt to embarrass my friend."

Lady Sylvia nodded in agreement, saying most reasonably, "I admit that it was a possibility," but then added with a hint of rebellion, "and if that was indeed the case, I dare say I would commend her for it."

"You would commend her?" Cedric found himself somewhat disoriented by the manner in which Lady Sylvia had altered their discussion.

"Yes, of course," she said frankly. "A woman cannot resort to uncivilized means to resolve her differences with a man as men frequently do. What recourse does a woman truly have to exact retribution from a man but to let the man make a fool of himself? In the present case, it would appear that Mr. Raith was most accommodating in respect of that opportunity."

"Then you will entertain no suggestion of censure for Miss Atwood?"

"No, no more than you have entertained censure for Mr. Raith."

"You think his flirtation is to be held as the equal of her conduct?" asked Mr. Stacey in the most incredulous of tones.

"No," replied Lady Sylvia, "not at all. I merely equate your familiarity of Mr. Raith with mine of Miss

Atwood. I accept your assessment of Mr. Raith, for I do not know him as you do. I merely ask that you respect my assessment of Miss Atwood, for you do not know her as I do."

Cedric turned sharply to look out the window, his jaw clinched against the frustration that exhorted him to chastise this obstinate woman. Her foolishness was more than apparent to himself, yet she would not be persuaded to abandon her associate to whom she had evidently extended her unreserved friendship. For that, at least, and for the good regard in which the late Sir Waverly always insisted upon her, she was to be respected. A truce, then, it must be.

"I trust," concluded Cedric in studied calm, "you shall do, in the end, what is right, as I have always known you to do, in whatever manner it shall evolve. On that confidence, I can and do entrust the affair, without prejudice, wholly to your judgment."

Chapter 14

The following afternoon at tea, a certain disquietude flitted annoyingly in Lady Sylvia's mind. Cedric and Mr. Raith had returned to London after suggesting they had been too long away from their business matters. Ariana and Gwyneth had excused themselves to confer with Carlton in the garden, citing the suitability of the lighting for their current effort. Only Isabella joined Lady Sylvia in the daily ritual of tea. The privacy of the moment invited the inquiring innocence of Isabella to be unrestrained in turning the conversation to the matter of Cedric and Ariana.

"I don't understand," said Isabella. "If Mr. Raith is responsible for what happened, why is Mr. Stacey so unpleasant with Ariana?"

"Cedric, I think, has always been leery of Ariana, or, rather, to be fair, he has been leery of the idea of Ariana. That is to say, anyone who might have been retained as my assistant and who was not a social equal would have caused the same apprehension in Cedric."

"But, could someone be your assistant and your equal at the same time?"

"A very apt question, my dear, and, no, probably not. I suspect it was that attitude that made them seem to be at odds from the very beginning. Because of that discord, I think Cedric must have viewed Ariana as something of an intruder."

"You mean like a thief?"

"Not precisely a thief; more like an unwelcome guest who comes uninvited, takes what you have to offer, and expects more, which sometimes amounts to the same thing as thievery."

Isabella regarded Lady Sylvia thoughtfully and then asked somewhat cautiously, "Do people think I am an intruder?"

"No, certainly not," responded Lady Sylvia firmly and without hesitation. "What life you have here I offered you freely and I give you freely with my most earnest endorsement. I should be deeply deprived if you were to choose not to live here."

Isabella frowned in her concentration to understand Lady Sylvia.

"I wonder," she began, with that facility of youth to change topics in mid-thought. "When they are together, they seem to be watchful of each other. They are loud when they talk, and they wave their hands about. They make me think," she said with only the slightest hint of humor, "of a bullfighter waving a cape to challenge the bull." Then in a more serious thought, she added, "It's as if they are fighting with each other, but they don't really want to be." She turned her furrowed eyebrows toward Lady Sylvia to ask, "Do you think that's possible?" Without waiting for a response, she abruptly changed directions again to remark, "Maybe it's not about being angry at all. Maybe they are really fighting for admiration."

As she paused to consider this thought, Lady Sylvia looked on Isabella with new admiration of her own and remarked, "There is very much to what you say." Taking up the thought, she observed, "People often express themselves not as they feel but as they think other people expect them to feel. Cedric, for one, is very sensitive to what people say about him and his family's honor. In somewhat the same way, Ariana is very keen on gaining approval for what she does or thinks. Indeed, I think Ariana looks upon approval as Cedric looks upon honor. That might explain why their conversations, even before there was cause for it, were rather vivid and intense. But if it is for admiration that they are fighting, then I fear they are fighting against themselves. True admiration is unguarded and can only be given and received without inhibition. I think it very likely that each wants to be admired by the other, but neither is willing to be unguarded enough to allow the other to say openly whether they do or don't for fear that they don't."

Chapter 15

On departing Southjoy Mission, Gavin took care to ensure that matters were quite settled between Cedric and himself. Their discourse as they rode, where opportunity permitted, was relaxed and free of discord. Cedric, by all appearances, had put the matter behind him, and from his easy manner, one could infer that it was supposed that Gavin would do likewise. To be certain that such was the case, Gavin lightly broached the subject of his embarrassment.

"I do sincerely hope," he remarked most casually, "that nothing untoward has come between you and Lady Sylvia because of my little incident with Miss Ariana Atwood."

Cedric, however, waved off any discussion of that account, noting, "Lady Sylvia is a remarkably sensible and resilient person, and though we do not always agree on all matters, we are never at odds about our differences." The mention of the incident, however, spurred Cedric to an additional thought. "What has most surprised me in this whole affair was how boldly Miss Atwood acted her part. It was certainly far more spirited than I would have expected of anyone in her station." After a moment, he commented further, "Yes, she has a boldness, indeed, that will bear some watching."

Noting Cedric's focus on Ariana rather than on himself, Gavin judged himself sufficiently reassured that he could venture to take his leave of Cedric to spend another day or two in Bath, citing a business opportunity that might be advantageous to his own resources.

"By all means," remarked Cedric, "and I am glad to see that you suffer no ill effect from your escapade."

And with that, Cedric continued on to London, while Gavin set about at once to attend to the matter on which he had been incessantly brooding since early morning.

Gavin chose an expedient post near the Pump Room where he could wait and watch for Mrs. Crandesol, it being common knowledge that she visited Bath Abbey nearly daily. Though she could not be considered as elevated in social class as Lady Sylvia, Mrs. Crandesol was, nonetheless, nearly as indomitable as Her Ladyship and would make a formidable ally in redressing the grievance that now occupied his thoughts. In the warmth of this day, good fortune smiled on his endeavor and did not cause him to wait overly long, for he had hardly settled himself to wait when he spied Mrs. Crandesol making a slow, unhurried exit from the Abbey. In his carefully confident manner, he approached Mrs. Crandesol, with no apparent agenda or intention of stopping, and greeted her in passing with, "A good day to you, m'lady," but then suddenly stopped.

"If I'm not mistaken," he said with pleasant surprise, "I have the honor of addressing Mrs. Crandesol of the Society of Native Architectures and Gardens!"

"Indeed, that is my name," she replied perfunctory, "and you," she asserted without hesitation, "are the oft noted associate of Mr. Stacey, if I have been properly informed."

"Indeed so! Mr. Gavin Raith, at your service, and allow me to say, I have heard much of, and admire, your good efforts to keep our shire beautiful."

"Indeed?" replied Mrs. Crandesol, her tone brimming with a certain doubtful challenge. "And would that include my declared and adamant opposition to that monstrosity of Southjoy Mission that is so recklessly championed by your friend's misguided aunt?"

Gavin smiled pleasantly.

"I can see that you are very well informed, but," he said frankly, "yes, as it happens, I am much in accord with your position as a matter of fact. I think it a most unfortunate obsession, this adoration of Sir Waverly Sylvia. It can lead to no good, you know, all that expense, all the unpleasantness. I fear even that Lady

Sylvia may find her fortune is not sufficient for the task. Mark my words. Sooner or later she will have to appeal to her nephew to meet her debts among all those workman, and there are a great many, you know."

Gavin smiled broadly.

"But who am I to be bothered by things that are none of my affair? Far be it from me to be spreading rumors of ill-fated enterprises."

His smile still broadly fixed upon his face, Gavin bid Mrs. Crandesol a good day and departed in the best of humor.

As he walked, Gavin could scarcely contain the urge to laugh, to let his laughter escape from deep within his lungs, to erupt without restraint until it filled the plaza with echoes of his retribution, for in his heart of hearts, he knew he had laid the scent of blood on the trail to Southjoy Mission, and hard upon it, the taste of prey would soon follow as surely as night follows after day. At the latter thought, he did laugh, a short, harsh laugh, for if, as purported by Mr. Cedric Stacey, Lady Sylvia shines as the light of day, then surely, as now primed by Mr. Gavin Raith, Mrs. Crandesol would loom forth as the dark of night, at least for Lady Sylvia.

A modest retribution, thought Gavin, *but retribution nonetheless*.

Chapter 16

Routine did not tarry overly long in returning to Southjoy Mission. The tensions of controversy were readily displaced by the concerted demands of the restoration, and memories of the social upheaval soon faded even from the servants' daily chatter. Fair weather guided workmen to apply their skilled labors to the renovation of the mansion's exterior and of the mansion's interior upon the intervention of foul weather. Supplies arrived daily along with a steady stream of new requisitions, and both hosts and staff were hard pressed to maintain their equanimity and efficiency amidst the effervescent workload.

If there was any perturbation of this idyllic commotion, it was a bothersome communication from Mr. Cunnings. Certain creditors had voiced a concern that Lady Sylvia was soon to be bankrupt and would be forfeit on her good faith commitments. How they arrived at this conjecture was left unsaid, but it befell Mr. Cunnings to allay their fears and, subsequently, to allay his own.

"I cannot say how such a rumor began," he wrote, "but I have, of course, set the matter to rights by denying it unreservedly. I trust this meets with your approval." Lady Sylvia had replied instantly that she most heartily endorsed his response and was most grateful for his diligence in the matter.

Such, however, was the momentum of the effort at Southjoy Mission that some considerable time, indeed, had lapsed since Lady Sylvia had undertaken a proper review of the accomplished and pending progress of the restoration. She wrote to Cedric frequently, of course, to describe their progress in general terms, but of late, Cedric's inquiries in reply were becoming more particular. He had not issued any complaint or belabored any concern, but there was a perceptible note of worry in his oft-repeated recommendation for cautious and prudent expenditures. Lady Sylvia was sensible to the practicality of this advice and, motivated by the communication from Mr. Cunnings, had seized upon a propitious moment to gather her ledgers, receipts, and sundry notes to reconcile her accounts and her recollections. She closeted herself in Sir Waverly's office, as she continued to call the study, and did not emerge again for some hours. When she did so, it was of a brevity sufficient only to summon Ariana, whereupon she returned to the seclusion of the study.

Ariana found her there, intently peering at the collection of documents as though trying to divine amongst their pages clues to a precious riddle.

"Lady Sylvia?" prompted Ariana softly.

Slowly, and with apparent reluctance, Lady Sylvia turned away from her notes and accounts to look vaguely in the direction of Ariana. Her eyes were unfocused, and her expression was lacking in vitality, suggesting that her thoughts were heavy with fatigue.

"Ariana," she began without inflection, "it seems our exuberance has exceeded our means."

Lady Sylvia focused her attention then to look at Ariana with the keenness of an observer watching an unfolding drama. She waited as possible repercussions flitted through Ariana's mind, each thought subtly reflected in a fleeting flicker of an eye or a slight, nearly imperceptible tilt of her head.

"Am I to understand—" asked Ariana presently.

"That I have spent more than good sense would endure?" interrupted Lady Sylvia with unflinching firmness. "Yes, that I have done, not so extreme as has been rumored, but perhaps more than would have been allowed by a more prudent perspective." As Ariana contemplated this reply, Lady Sylvia continued with undiminished firmness, "Cedric must not know."

Ariana's eyes quickly found those of Lady Sylvia, and for some seconds their eyes locked intently in a shared vision of Mr. Stacey's censure. Neither doubted the scorn and disapproval that would be forthcoming. Ariana nodded slowly to indicate that she understood.

She glanced at the papers spread on the desk and then nodded again that she agreed. Turning back to Lady Sylvia, she asked, "What is to be done?"

Lady Sylvia smiled warmly at Ariana.

"Your enthusiasm revives my very spirit," she said with sincere appreciation. "So, I shall keep nothing from you." She motioned toward the desk. "These ledgers and notes bear all the facts, what we have spent, what remains to be spent, and what resources I have. I give you leave to examine them in detail because you must know all there is. Then together perhaps we can salvage our effort from its impending ruin."

Nearly two hours passed as Lady Sylvia, with unswerving focus, guided Ariana through the collective details of incomes and expenditures, pausing only to debate economies of effort. At length, Lady Sylvia concluded, "So you see the problem. If we suspend work for a time, we will conserve our funds, but we would risk the loss of Cedric's endorsement. I fear, with greater certainty, our creditors, who already have been incited to uneasiness for whatever reason, would not hesitate to express their concerns to Mr. Stacey. Such embarrassment would not easily be born by Cedric, nor would it rest easily on my conscience."

"We are agreed," said Ariana, returning yet again to the basic problem, "the issue is economy." She addressed Lady Sylvia with resolute practicality. "Even if expenditures are reduced to the very minimum, the sad truth is, you need more money for the commitments already underway, especially if they sustain the fair rate of progress already established. I think we must consider how that might be achieved."

A hint of fear was perceptible in Lady Sylvia's expression. "But, my dear, what options do I have other than asking Cedric? And you know I cannot do that."

"No, asking Mr. Stacey will not do," said Ariana flatly. "I can think of only three ways open to a woman of independent means, if she desires to retain her independence: sell property, let property for a period of time, or invest funds for a profit as businessmen do or such as might be accomplished through a bank."

"Usury?" interjected Lady Sylvia. "That is out of the question." Her tone left no doubt.

"It would not have to be usury, but I confess, I have no knowledge of how business investments work or how long it takes for them to succeed. So we are left with selling or letting." She glanced somewhat appraisingly as she asked, "I presume you would not care to consider selling any parcel of land belonging to Southjoy Mission?"

Lady Sylvia was unequivocal. "No. That would suggest that the very project we are pursuing is in distress. Besides, you must remember that Southjoy Mission and all of its holdings were entailed to Cedric, and he retains title to them."

"Yes, I beg your pardon, Lady Sylvia. I had quite forgotten," apologized Ariana.

"As to letting any part of Southjoy Mission," continued Lady Sylvia, "I am sure Cedric would frown on the idea."

Ariana brightened with a look of spirited enterprise. "Then we must find a way to convince Mr. Stacey that it is practical and desirable."

"Ariana, my dear, might I hope you have a particular scheme in mind?"

"I do," said Ariana with enthusiasm. "There are two rather large tracks of land that stand idle where neighboring fields are being prosperously farmed. Whenever I have had occasion to pass near them, I have had the amusing thought that they were longing to be put to some good use, and I think the current situation is the perfect opportunity for that use to be found. If you were to let those fields for farming or grazing, you might collect a handsome fee."

Her eyes sparkled anew as she rushed on with a further thought.

"It would stand us in good stead with our neighbors too. We could say that we want Southjoy Mission to contribute to the vitality of the community, and what better way than that the community should come to regard Southjoy Mission as a source of profit for themselves?"

"I see, yes," said Lady Sylvia, "and it is the kind of proposal that Cedric would find both sensible and appropriate for an estate. What's more, and importantly so, it would be an undertaking for the benefit of the estate and not for any profit to me personally." Cautiously, then, she asked, "But, how would we go about doing such a thing? Where would we begin?"

"We would certainly need to have those questions answered before approaching Mr. Stacey," said Ariana thoughtfully. "Perhaps Mr. Cunnings would be a valuable guide in this matter."

"Yes," agreed Lady Sylvia, "very good indeed. He is rather clever with such matters. But," she paused to emphasize her position, "it must be you, Ariana, who contacts him, and there must be no hint of urgency, no sense of anything indelicate."

"Yes, most certainly that," replied Ariana. She smiled then as she said, "I think it can be done without difficulty. I shall approach Mr. Cunnings and inquire if we might have the benefit of his advice. I shall explain to him that Southjoy Mission has too long stood apart from the community, and we are exploring ways to dissolve that separation. I'm sure he will find the idea appealing to him and readily offer his service."

"He will indeed." Lady Sylvia brightened considerably at this thought. It was a plan of sensible bearing, yet bold enough that even Sir Waverly might have thought well of it.

"Nothing untoward should be discerned in such a request, and I suspect Mr. Cunnings is clever enough to understand that there would be a commission for himself in this venture."

"If, for whatever reason, anything confidential should arise," added Ariana, "I am sure we can rely on Mr. Cunnings's discretion as well."

"I am very much persuaded to the soundness and suitability of your proposal," concluded Lady Sylvia, "and I confess it endows me with a measure of confidence I could not have managed alone." Her spirit renewed, she said decisively, "I give you leave to contact Mr. Cunnings, to seek his advice, and most certainly to explore the possibility to its fullest."

The interview with Mr. Cunnings was most congenial. Ariana had arranged to spend the better part of a day in Bath, and when she inquired as to the opportunity to be received by Mr. Cunnings for a bit of advice, he was most agreeable. Upon hearing the proposal, he was, of course, pleased that he could be of service to Lady Sylvia.

"It is an admirable proposal," he said with enthusiasm and went so far as to offer to make suitable inquiries "to ascertain who might regard this handsome prospect favorably." He added, "I shall indicate that we are exploring how this land might be used to the mutual benefit and advantage of all parties. That should afford me an opportunity to distinguish between reliable interest and mere curiosity." It was a pleasing way to indicate that all manner of discretion in the matter was fully understood, and with that assurance, Ariana concluded with some comfortable degree of confidence that the matter could well be entrusted without reservation to Mr. Cunnings's capable attention.

Relieved that her enterprise had begun so admirably, Ariana experienced a certain gaiety in the success of her venture. As she took her leave of Mr. Cunnings, she was delighted further to find Mr. Cunnings's son, Andrew, at hand in the outer office.

"Dear Andrew," she exclaimed, "I had so hoped I might have the pleasure of seeing you during my visit here."

"Miss Ariana," Andrew responded with genuine delight of his own, "but it is I who must claim the greater part of the pleasure in such a glad meeting, for I have frequently thought about your grand effort at Southjoy Mission, and I must confess, I am much in want of news of your progress."

"And perhaps of Miss Isabella, also?" Ariana ventured to ask in the spontaneity spawned by her good humor. "For she asked particularly to be remembered to you, if I should happen to see you."

Andrew's broad smile said much in reply.

"That she should remember me is more privilege than I dared to hope."

"I believe I can say sincerely that she remembers you most fondly, as do we all, of course. If it would please you and if you might have a moment to spare, I should be glad to share with you whatever small news I might have."

"If I did not have such a moment," said Andrew with good humor, "I should endeavor to make one instantly. Indeed, if I might further suggest, perhaps you would find a cup of tea suitably refreshing before you return to Southjoy Mission?"

"I should very much enjoy a cup of tea," replied Ariana, "and had you not recommended it, I do believe I would have made so bold as to suggest it myself."

All parties being suitably pleased by this arrangement, Ariana and Andrew set off in search of an agreeable place for tea and, of course, amiable discourse. As they walked, Andrew offered that a freshly baked Sally Lunn bun might elevate the pleasure of the tea to a memorable delight.

"A wonderful thought," replied Ariana with her warmest smile. "Nothing could be more excellent."

The tearoom was still busy at that hour. The tables being nearly filled with patrons, the room itself was filled with a certain frenetic activity that enfolded and wrapped about Ariana with the same comforting effect as when a weary body takes to the warm healing waters of the spa. For a moment, Ariana closed her eyes and let the sounds of the tearoom meld into a faraway hum. Andrew, as young men are wont to do, was speaking of himself and of his future. His demeanor, though, was soft, and his gentle voice floated above the din like the comforting sound of waves lapping in rhythmic rhymes against a sandy shore. Ariana accepted it all as a soothing balm layered gently upon her spirit. She smiled then unconsciously as she observed to herself how well the mild and unpretentious manner of Andrew would accommodate his entry into the clergy. It was a rare gift in a world where strife seemed less far away than it used to be. There was much need for quiet confidence, and even now Ariana welcomed it as she smiled again at Andrew.

"If you will pardon the observation, Miss Ariana," remarked Andrew, "you seem to be in rather exceedingly good spirit, almost as though something untoward has been made exceedingly right."

"Indeed," replied Ariana, "at this moment, I am so exceedingly diverted by pleasure that no difficulty can assail my humor nor detract from it in any way."

Mr. Cunnings was occupied with writing a brief note in one of his many journals when Andrew returned to his office.

"I trust Miss Atwood is safely on her way back to Southjoy Mission," remarked Mr. Cunnings by way of greeting.

"She is," replied Andrew. "I, myself, saw her to her coach immediately after what I believe was a most satisfactory tea, and, I dare say, Miss Atwood thought as much herself. 'No difficulty can assail the pleasure of this moment' is how she put it, if I remember correctly."

Mr. Cunnings looked up from his journal, his business acumen alerted by such an innocent observation, especially by a young man not too well acquainted with difficulties himself. Phrasing his question in his much practiced tone of indifference, he asked, "And was there a particular difficulty?"

"Now that you ask, it did seem a rather curious comment, but, no, she addressed no difficulty at all. Though," he hurried on, "it did seem rather to me that she was relieved about something."

"I wonder," said Mr. Cunnings, speaking more to himself than to Andrew and undoubtedly recalling a certain recent rumor, "I wonder if there is something more to this proposal to let parcels of land than was discussed with me. If so, then it may be of some greater urgency than I had initially supposed. Indeed, it must be so," he said thoughtfully, "or she would not have sent her personal envoy to seek me out so particularly."

Chapter 17

Mr. Cunnings's attention to detail was unsurpassed in the business world of Bath, and in a matter of some urgency regarding the affairs of Lady Sylvia, he redoubled his effort. In less than a fortnight, he had assembled several interesting prospects, and had he not the obligation of a pressing matter in London, he would have finalized the arrangements immediately. Alas, he could not delay his departure to London and had to content himself with an optimistic report of the imminent and favorable prospects, which he conveyed to Southjoy Mission by means of Andrew.

Andrew accepted the task eagerly and set off for Southjoy Mission the next morning. Upon his arrival, he was delighted to find that the news he bore was welcomed by Lady Sylvia with much glad relief, to the extent that Andrew himself was welcomed with a greater degree of genuine cordiality than a more common occasion might otherwise warrant. Indeed, it was cause enough to impart decidedly good spirits to everyone at Southjoy Mission.

"Lady Sylvia," asked Isabella after ample courtesy and courteous conversation, "may I show Andrew my flower garden? The blossoms are so beautiful just now."

"Yes, of course," granted Lady Sylvia in the pleasantness of the moment, "and then you may join us in the sitting room for refreshments. Ariana and I should finish our task in but a few moments, and Gwyneth will join us momentarily, I should think. With good fortune, Carlton will be ready for some refreshment soon too."

"I should like that very much," acknowledged Andrew, as Isabella, glad of the opportunity, cheerfully led the way to the garden. Though the day was already warming to a swelter, the brightness of the sky seemed to impart a certain lightness to their steps.

"And are you happy here?" Andrew asked, as they walked through the garden. "I am most anxious that you should be," he added with a certain boldness that seemed pleasing to Isabella, for she smiled warmly in return of Andrew's intense regard of herself.

"Exceedingly," she replied. "I have had many occasions to think of it, and I believe I am the most fortunate of people." She paused pensively and then said with some little intensity, "And it isn't just the warmth of home that I feel but also that I am adding to its warmth. I know it may sound strange, but sometimes I feel that Southjoy Mission itself is alive. Oh, I know that it isn't," she added quickly, "but that's how it seems. It's as though it has been ill for a very long time, and now we are, all of us here, helping it to get well."

She laughed lightly then and scolded herself, saying, "You probably think that's childish of me, and now you will make fun of me."

"No!" protested Andrew. "I would never make fun of you! You are so—" He stopped suddenly, aware of what he was about to say and embarrassed by the presumption.

They looked at one another for a second or two, suspended in the absence of words, and then both laughed warmly.

"Thank you," said Isabella warmly.

Andrew, still wrapped in the confusion and the delight of his boldness, could only manage to begin to say, "I didn't, that is, I—" but stopped at once, for in the sincerity of his mind, any remark his thoughts would permit him at that instant could but compound his presumption.

"Thank you for your kindness," said Isabella, coming to his rescue, "for what you said, and," she added coquettishly, "maybe for what you didn't say too."

Andrew was about to protest again but was spared the necessity as Isabella graciously turned away, permitting him to recover.

She gestured as she turned, saying, "It is a grand estate, don't you think? One day all will be beautiful here."

Andrew gratefully nodded his agreement, adding, "It undoubtedly will be very beautiful. There is much to be done yet, of course, but Father tells me there has been such notable progress in such a very short time that all of you are to be much congratulated, for it is truly a most remarkable accomplishment."

"Thank you again," said Isabella, "but what credit there may be is mostly due Ariana. Lady Sylvia would say as much without hesitation."

"And Mr. Stacey must be quite proud too, I should think," said Andrew.

Isabella gave that thought some brief consideration and then said, "Perhaps, but sometimes it's hard to understand Mr. Stacey. He is proud, that is certain, but of what he is proud, that is not always clear."

Somewhat apologetic, Andrew ventured, "I have heard that Mr. Stacey is not fond of Miss Ariana—just idle gossip, of course, but," he added more optimistically, "if that is the case, perhaps he will think better of her when he sees how successfully she has worked to give other people a better opinion of Southjoy Mission."

"I hope it is so," said Isabella, "because I am persuaded, in spite of appearances, that if they could let their hearts speak, they would speak of nothing but their finest regard for each other."

"I understand what you mean," remarked Andrew. "To speak what is truly in one's heart sometimes demands a moral courage that differs from the courage of confrontation. Unfortunately, we tend to be more schooled in the latter than in the former, so much so that some people require struggles or moral dilemmas to enable their characters to express themselves truly, to permit them to grow, and perhaps even to expand enough to recognize the needs of other people. Maybe Mr. Stacey and Miss Ariana are like that, and they create their own struggles so that, in a sense, they can find a mutually comfortable way to engage each other." Seeing the frown on Isabella's face, Andrew quickly rejected his own thought. "You are quite right," he rebuffed himself. "People of the merit of Mr. Stacey and Miss Ariana are well adept at recognizing the needs of others. But," he added, "it might make some sense in the matter of injustice. As unfortunate as it may be, I have known people who were much esteemed by society but who could not find it in themselves to comprehend fairness until they felt the lack of it for themselves."

Isabella looked toward Andrew with an air of thoughtful sadness.

"Then Ariana must understand it beyond all people," she said, "and Mr. Stacey not at all." Suddenly stricken by the effrontery of her remark, she said most urgently, "Forgive me. That was most unkind of me. I beg you not to remember it."

With the gentle kindness of understanding, Andrew remarked, "You must care a great deal for her."

"I do," admitted Isabella. "Ariana and Gwyneth are like very dear sisters to me. They include me in everything, and in nothing do they ever keep me at a distance. They and Lady Sylvia are my family, as true a family as anyone might have."

"Then," said Andrew softly, "they are as much to be envied as are you, for surely they must regard you as much a treasure for themselves as you, indeed, regard them for yourself."

In the softness of the gentle silence that followed, they turned to stroll slowly through the remainder of the garden, the empathy of their spirits sufficing to imbue a certain synchronization to their steps and a pleasantness to their smiles.

Chapter 18

Mr. Cunnings consoled himself with the knowledge that his untimely trip to London would, at least, afford him an opportunity to address a courtesy call upon Mr. Stacey, who had, after all, asked him to be mindful of the affairs of Southjoy Mission.

"Should there arise any development of particular interest," Mr. Stacey had said, "I would value your impartial view of it."

In the commonplace endeavors of man and state, developments of notable merit are a genuine rarity, and one whose importance is only subtly discernible, as at present, is rarer still.

Upon his arrival, Mr. Stacey extended a welcome to Mr. Cunnings of such congeniality as to embolden Mr. Cunnings with a certain confidence of purpose. Such was the assurance of his position that when he had completed his report to Mr. Stacey, with particular emphasis on the letting of two fields at Southjoy Mission, he beamed a broad smile of self-congratulatory satisfaction toward Mr. Stacey in anticipation, no doubt, of the expression of gratitude that surely would be forthcoming from that astute gentleman known for his generosity. As regards any hint of enthusiasm, however, there was none. Mr. Stacey peered at Mr. Cunnings for a very long second with no expression at all. Then in the softest of voices, much like the whisper of distant thunder, he inquired of Mr. Cunnings, "Perhaps you could elaborate on this," he hesitated and then continued, "this new enterprise?"

"Of course," said Mr. Cunnings hastily, himself astute enough to see that Mr. Stacey had not been previously apprised of this affair. As the sense of a gathering storm began to permeate the room, Mr. Cunnings concluded that clarity with respect to what he knew precisely, particularly with respect to his own actions, might yet stand him in good stead with Mr. Stacey and, perhaps, even preserve for himself what pardon might prove necessary for any indiscretion with respect to Lady Sylvia.

"Well, then," he began, "I first learned of this proposal when Miss Ariana Atwood approached me to inquire of my opinion as to its merits and likelihood of success."

"Miss Atwood, you say," said Mr. Stacey. "Then Lady Sylvia was not present."

"No, Miss Atwood came to me alone. Indeed, as of the present moment, I have not had occasion to speak with Lady Sylvia on this matter at all, it being left apparently to Miss Atwood's discretion. She was, however, most particular to assure me that Lady Sylvia endorsed the proposal without reservation."

"No doubt," said Mr. Stacey, "and was there no indication of motivation for this rather unusual course of action?"

Mr. Cunnings sought to address his reply in those comforting tones of reason and careful deliberation that are so often advisable in delicate negotiations. "Miss Atwood said it would help to show people that Southjoy Mission could contribute favorably to the local economy, which, in turn, would encourage them to view Southjoy Mission itself more favorably. Beyond that," he noted thoughtfully, "nothing further was suggested directly on the subject."

"Then something was suggested indirectly?" asked Mr. Stacey, ever attentive to the least of nuances that hinted at what he wanted to hear.

"Not to me personally, but Miss Atwood did make a comment to my son, Andrew, which, when heard out of context, suggested that there was more urgency to the affair than Miss Atwood had stated explicitly. That, coupled with the persistent rumor of financial difficulty, which Lady Sylvia personally dispelled unreservedly, persuaded me to act on the matter with some degree of diligence on my own part."

Mr. Cunnings then related what had been reported to him by Andrew and then spoke in some detail as to his contacts and potential arrangements on behalf of

Lady Sylvia. When he had exhausted his knowledge of the affair, Mr. Stacey thanked him warmly, as one thanks a friend or a respected confidant.

"You have done well in this matter, and I am grateful for the fullness of your report."

If Mr. Stacey had any reservation regarding what he had just heard, it was not evident in his manner, and Mr. Cunnings was able to take his leave with a sense, if not quite of satisfaction, at least of relief.

Cedric appeared to be preoccupied when Gavin arrived. Summoned in a manner that suggested some urgency, Gavin now sat comfortably in Cedric's office displaying the amused indifference that had charmed Cedric early in their youthful school days. Their friendship had easily weathered the fiasco at Southjoy Mission, and, indeed, precisely because of that embarrassment, Cedric was confident that no one would be more aptly suited than Mr. Raith for the undertaking that he now contemplated, inspired by the revelations of Mr. Cunnings's report.

"Miss Atwood is not immune to the benefits of position, I should think," said Gavin with feigned impartiality. "It would not be the first time that profit for a neighbor meant profit for a servant."

"Just so," replied Cedric without conviction, "but I rather think she inclines a bit toward puritanical ideals, despite her practicality. I am persuaded that her prudent nature is not amenable to temptations of that sort."

"And what sort of temptation would appeal to a prudent puritan?" asked Gavin with genuine interest.

"Ambition," replied Cedric, his tone firm and unequivocal in its conviction. "Ambition knows no provenance. It recognizes none, and it respects none."

"Ambition! Well, well," said Gavin with a hint of admiration only vaguely concealed in the gusto with which he took up the accusation. He squared himself in his chair to look earnestly at Cedric. "I believe you have it exactly. Ambition would do very nicely for someone who wanted her betters to take notice of her."

"I have had occasion to think as much in the past," remarked Cedric flatly.

Gavin smiled wryly, like someone who has just seen through a ruse and appreciated its peculiar advantage.

"The appearance of influence," he offered, "can be very persuasive to a gentleman if he is occupied with his own ambition, especially when beauty is lacking or maybe even because of it."

Cedric was silent a moment, impassive, not quite ready to pass judgment.

"So, then, we are thinking that Miss Atwood has designs on the conquest of some gentleman?" he asked, seeking confirmation.

"I am as much persuaded to that opinion as you are," replied Gavin with the confidence of one who sees a matter already decided and has nothing to gain by contradicting it.

Cedric's sigh came with a sense of frustration.

"This is, at present, nothing but coarse speculation on our part, rational enough to put us on guard, but not sufficient to support the condemnation of any act she may have taken with or without authority." He added, "We must remember, too, that Lady Sylvia is due unreserved respect, and out of that respect for her, I would not want to be the cause of injury in this matter without undeniable foundation."

Gavin cocked his head slightly to one side as a glimmer of understanding began to shimmer in his mind.

"And that is why you have summoned me," he said slowly with a mixture of pleasure and bemusement. "I am to make the foundation undeniable."

Cedric peered sternly at his friend. "You are to discover it if it is there to be found."

Gavin gave a slight bow of his head to acknowledge his understanding of the distinction, if not the censure, in his friend's remark. "If there is aught to be found, I shall have it. Depend upon it. I shall seize it—as surely as honor would requite a debt."

Retrieving a small leather satchel from his desk and handing it to Gavin, Cedric concluded, "You will find ample funds here for whatever expenses might befall you, along with a note of no particular significance for you to carry to Lady Sylvia. That should provide you with reason enough to visit Southjoy Mission if it suits your purpose to do so. You will say simply that since you were to be nearby, I entreated you to deliver it. The rest I leave to your resourcefulness."

Chapter 19

The journey to Bath provided Mr. Gavin Raith abundant opportunity to contemplate the circumstances that led Ariana Atwood to approach Mr. Cunnings. He dismissed the possibility that Ariana was looking for personal gain, and he was certain that Cedric did not entertain that notion either. It was, however, the kind of precipitous undertaking that the want of ready funds had been known to cause. On that subject, Mr. Gavin Raith was well informed. In the present instance, it was cause enough for him to marvel at the possibility that the seed of monetary concern he had sown with Mrs. Crandesol might actually bear a bountiful fruit of social discontent. The thought of it buoyed his spirit considerably.

The last time Gavin Raith savored an event that could be called a success was at university. Then, he had been motivated. Whether it was vengeance or a debt of gratitude, he could not remember, but motivated he was nonetheless. In what he considered to be his most memorable scheme, he had netted a rather handsome profit—not so handsome as to speak of wealth, of course, but enough that an impoverished student might feel the heady inebriation of success. A far greater profit dating from that time, and more useful, was the favorable regard of Mr. Cedric Stacey. That alone had gained him entry into financial circles that would otherwise have been closed to him. Through them, he had accrued small sums here and there, not enough for independence, but sufficient to stay near enough by that he could on occasion benefit from his advantageous association with Cedric Stacey. Only occasionally had he been seized with a twinge of resentment that it should be his lot to be content with the scraps and table droppings from his master's feast. Such moments of resentment, though, were quickly dispelled by his propensity for indebtedness and the accompanying need for funds to pay those debts, and now that Cedric had ascended into the ranks of the very wealthy, far more financial doors were opening to him than ever before. Unfortunately for Gavin Raith, where treasuries are deep, thieves are thick.

Behind one such door, Gavin Raith encountered wits far sharper than his own with the result that he had been convinced by a deceit that surpassed his own imagination to invest in a fledgling company that reputedly would reap him a vast profit. Of course, to reap a profit of such magnitude, it was absolutely necessary to act on the instant. Convinced of his own cleverness, he invested all that he could amass on short order. Alas, to date, Gavin had naught but slips of paper to attest to his investment, and of fortune, there was but rumor of imminent collapse and, therein, the image of his own financial ruin.

He had, numerous times, thought of appealing to Cedric for aid in this matter, but, knowing the limits of Cedric's tolerance, he had ultimately dismissed the idea. It was upon the relentless approach of this calamity that he was brooding darkly when he received the summons from Cedric. Not one to leave a stone unturned when a nugget of gold could be lurking behind it, Gavin readily welcomed the diversion to Bath where he might hope to find people more amenable to his singular talents than he had encountered of late in London.

It was, in truth, not a difficult task. A few brief words with a very eager Mr. Cunnings were sufficient. Mr. Cunnings was still suffering from a hint of guilt over his unintended revelation of Lady Sylvia's plan to Mr. Stacey. He eagerly directed Gavin toward certain trades people who would be ready to extol the virtues of their work at Southjoy Mission. It was, after all, a common aspect of human nature to want the accolades, however superficial, of any superior, and a hearty, "Well done, my good man," had loosened many tighter tongues than this lot would have. It was, therefore, not long before Gavin Raith had extolled his way to a rather comprehensive picture of the undertakings at

Southjoy Mission, and from the information so readily volunteered, it was apparent that Lady Sylvia was attempting to do a rather excessive amount of renovation in a very short time. Already there were carpenters, brick layers, and cabinet makers, along with rumors of custom furnishings, special fabrics, tapestries, and draperies, and even an artist to render it all appealing. If his estimates were even roughly accurate, the rate of expenditure would be difficult for Lady Sylvia to sustain without Cedric's intervention, even with the modest wealth that was at hand to her own discretion, all quite in accordance with his suspicions as to the want of funds.

Complete confirmation of his assessment awaited him at Southjoy Mission, of this he was certain. In his own mind, he was beginning to perceive an element of stealth in the affairs of Southjoy Mission, and where there was stealth, there was always vulnerability. His mind began to swirl with possibilities. He would go to Southjoy Mission, and on this occasion, there would be no arrogant disregard directed upon himself, no unmitigated disdain; he would not permit it. If need be, it would be his pleasure to judiciously apply a slight irritation to Lady Sylvia's pride and the conflict that it must now be suffering with her increasingly vulnerable finances; that, he was convinced, would be sufficient to quell any disrespect from that quarter.

As he contemplated this turn of events and of his fortunes, he marveled at his own resourcefulness. He reveled in a vision of his own superiority in which he commanded servitude and obedience even from the likes of Lady Sylvia, and in these palpitating machinations of his mind, he began to perceive a solution of solutions and, perhaps, even a vengeance of vengeances.

"This will do very nicely," he said, as he examined the stylish carriage hired to take him to Southjoy Mission. If the plan he was formulating moment by moment was to succeed, it would be advantageous to present himself gilded with the appearance of success, which, as is well known, can excite confidence where none is due.

Gavin took special care to ensure that his approach to Southjoy Mission was noted sufficiently in advance of his arrival as to cause a stir among the servants and to incite an anxious level of anticipation among its occupants. He brought the carriage to a complete stop to take a long, unhurried look at the mansion and then proceeded at a most leisurely pace.

A servant greeted him on the instant of his arrival and took him without delay to the sitting room where Lady Sylvia awaited him.

"Lady Sylvia," he said in his most sincere tone, "I hope my unexpected visit to Southjoy Mission will not be received as an unwelcome intrusion. I come bearing a message from Mr. Stacey."

The cordiality of his greeting was reciprocated by Lady Sylvia most civilly, albeit with a tone brimming with curiosity.

"Mr. Raith, it is a pleasure to see you again, and of course visitors are always welcome at Southjoy Mission. You need not come with the obligation of a messenger," she added, matching his sincerity, "but as you have, I must hope it is not a matter of such urgency that Cedric imposed on his friend to deliver it?"

"Not at all, Lady Sylvia," said Gavin most comfortably. "It was merely that I was to be nearby, and Cedric thought to take advantage of my proximity."

"How fortunate," she said, not quite relieved of the hint of anxiety that Mr. Raith inspired. Tea was brought in just then, providing a few welcome moments of proper social routine to further quell the lingering sense of unpleasant foreboding that persisted in nagging at her thoughts. She was, perhaps, more ill at ease than usual owing to the absence of Ariana, who was, at present, occupied with tasks that required her undivided attention.

As they settled comfortably with tea, she inquired, "And is it business or pleasure that lures you from London?"

"A small matter of business, as it happens, but if I may say," he added in his most agreeable manner, "I need not be lured from London to spend time in the country. In truth, I am fonder of the country than most of my associates expect of a Londoner. Indeed, it may soon be that I will spend more time in the country than in London," said Gavin, in a tone that invited Lady Sylvia to inquire as to how that may be.

"Well," said Gavin with some hesitation. "Well, yes, I think I may tell you," he said, emphasizing "you." "It has been my good luck, for I can claim no other merit to my fate in this matter than luck—luck, I say—to learn of an unusually splendid investment, one that may very soon reap a huge fortune in return." His jubilant smile suddenly turned to apprehension as he added earnestly, "You understand, of course, this is all tête-à-tête between us only."

"Of course," said Lady Sylvia in her most confidential manner. "I shall be most particular to say nothing of it. But do tell me, you have so keenly piqued my interest, what is the nature of this venture that it can produce such a handsome reward?"

"Indeed, Lady Sylvia, that is an excellent question, one that I myself asked at once upon hearing of its possibility, and I shall tell you what was told me. What transforms this investment from the ordinary to the extraordinary is not so much the object of the investment itself but rather the location of the investment. You see, the company in question is situated in South Africa."

"South Africa," declared Lady Sylvia dubiously. "I cannot recall at this moment any acquaintance who has ever been to South Africa."

"Indeed. Again, Lady Sylvia, I do believe you have a natural gift for understanding the essence of the opportunity. No one much thinks of South Africa except that it is uncivilized and completely unsuited to commerce. You might recall that there were some coastal outposts established early on whose purpose was merely to supply commercial shipping vessels with vegetables and such. Even such innocuous efforts, however, were difficult to maintain and often were subject to violent attacks by local tribesmen. So, indeed, South Africa does not readily come to mind when one thinks of investments."

"I believe there were good reasons for some of those attacks," said Lady Sylvia, without being overly judgmental. "But, if I understand you correctly, there must now be a way to bridge the conflict between foreigners and natives?"

"Exactly so, and it is the most natural of bridges. To put it simply, they have something we want, but we have something they want even more, and they are willing to trade for it advantageously to us. In a word, what they have is ivory."

He pronounced the word slowly, enunciating each syllable as though it were a delicacy to be savored, and to sweep away any question Lady Sylvia might have had about his sensibility, he emphasized the confidence of his declaration with his broadest, most engaging smile.

"Ivory," he repeated, "prized for its delicate color, its luster, and its remarkably smooth texture."

"I can appreciate the value of ivory," said Lady Sylvia, "but why, then, should this trade be arranged so secretively?"

Gavin glanced at Lady Sylvia with a countenance that could equally well have been admiration or frustration, but when he spoke, it was in the tone of unperturbed rationality.

"Lady Sylvia, if I may be permitted to observe, moment by moment, I understand increasingly well why Cedric holds you in such unusually high esteem. You have the gift of understanding these affairs in fine detail, and when you have not the clarity you desire, you seek it on the instant. Admirable, most admirable."

He paused to consider his response and then addressed Lady Sylvia in the manner of discussing business with one of his colleagues.

"It seems, Lady Sylvia, even in a region as remote and as undeveloped as South Africa, people can be dissatisfied with their superiors. Groups are organizing to oppose the ruling class, who may well be nothing but ruffians themselves. Be that as it may, opposition of that magnitude requires funds, weapons, ammunition, and influence, all arranged, needless to say, without the knowledge of those who might not want to be deposed."

"But this cannot be legal," objected Lady Sylvia.

"Lady Sylvia," said Gavin with proper indignation, "who are we to judge them when we know so very little about them? If there were no grievances, surely there would be no protests." Softening his tone again, he added, "Besides, the transactions themselves are quite legal, and, if we are to remain aloof from their petty squabbles and not interfere with the proper deliberations of what is rightly their own society, then that is as far as we may inquire."

"Yes, I see that," said Lady Sylvia without conviction, "and you are very much persuaded that you shall have a return on your investment in the very near future?"

The tenacity of Lady Sylvia's attention to the potential for profit caused Gavin to sit back, confident now and assured of his position.

"I am very sure of it," he said pleasantly.

"Mr. Raith," asked Lady Sylvia, herself now sitting forward, "if someone were to hear of this opportunity, say, from a respected friend, do you think it would be possible for him, or her for that matter, to add to this investment?"

Gavin pursed his lips, less to suggest consideration than to suppress the exhilaration that threatened to overrun his controlled demeanor as his prey so nonchalantly strayed into his baited snare.

"Lady Sylvia," he asked cautiously, "am I to understand that you would entertain the notion of investing in this venture even with the risks you have already perceived?"

"I must admit I am intrigued by the possibility," replied Lady Sylvia, "and were the way open to me, I believe that I might be so inclined, yes."

Gavin smiled engagingly. "Once again, you have managed to impress me with your incisive thinking, and that makes three times in one conversation. I know hardly a man, let alone a woman, who has done the same." He frowned, then, in concentration, saying soberly, "Let me think a moment." However, scarcely had he paused when he brightened and said in a tone as staid as any matter of business could be addressed, "I believe there is a way, and if you would care to leave it to me, it would be my greatest pleasure to make the necessary arrangements. But, mind you," he added cautiously, "it is a delicate matter. Not a word of this to anyone, to anyone at all."

The euphoria experienced by Mr. Gavin Raith at this turn of events, so cleverly engineered, propelled him to London with the greatest of expedience with only a brief diversion to Bath. Ensuring that he was sufficiently discreet and circumspect that Cedric Stacey should not know of his return to London, Gavin adroitly retrieved the ivory shares that he would now convey to Lady Sylvia. Upon the instant, he hastened to retrace his steps to Bath.

He had left word in Bath to be delivered to Lady Sylvia ahead of his return, instructing her as to a rendezvous with him at the Pump Room where, in spite of or because of, its public openness, their transaction could be completed with the utmost discretion. Gavin, himself, made certain that he arrived early so that he might, at the appointed time, beam his most gracious smile at Lady Sylvia as she approached him with exact punctuality. "Lady Sylvia," he said by way of greeting, "it is a most propitious day."

"Mr. Raith," she replied, "it has been my fervent hope that it would be so." As they settled into the chairs of a well-situated table, she asked, "Was there much difficulty obtaining the shares?"

"I was required to pursue a path less direct than I might have wished," he replied pleasantly, "but in all negotiations, there is inevitably some give and take, some intrigue, a certain need for discretion. Suffice it to say that I succeeded, and, indeed, here are the very shares for your inspection."

Reaching across the table, Lady Sylvia took the proffered parcel from Gavin's hand, opened it carefully, and studiously examined its content. After only a moment, an anxious exhilaration caused her to inhale deeply. Then, addressing Gavin, she admitted, "These shares mean more to me than you may suspect, and I am most grateful to you, most grateful indeed." Handing him in return a small pouch of no great distinction, she said, "It seems so pedestrian after the service you have performed, but I think you will find here ample funds, as we had discussed, to account for these shares, along with an additional amount to cover the expenses you no doubt encountered in acquiring them."

Gavin smiled broadly and took this opportunity to hand Lady Sylvia a glass of the natural spa water from the King's Spring he had ordered for just this moment. Lifting his own glass, he intoned, "A toast, Lady Sylvia. May these shares profit you as much as the satisfaction I see on your face profits me." Taking a swallow of the warm mineral water, he added with a grimace given in good humor, "And may pungently piquant waters always betide you good health."

Having thus concluded their transaction in the most amiable of fashions, Gavin admonished Lady Sylvia as he took his leave, "Guard your shares securely and away from prying eyes."

Lady Sylvia assured him that she would do so with great diligence and again expressed her appreciation for his most generous and expeditious consideration. To any casual observer, Lady Sylvia and Gavin Raith could easily have been mistaken as the quintessential picture of a matronly aunt and a devoted nephew.

"I should not be surprised if it were quite soon," said Gavin casually.

"But surely," suggested Mrs. Crandesol, "Lady Sylvia has given her assurance to Mr. Cunnings that all is quite well. The workmen are satisfied, and all that atrocious reconstruction continues."

"Mr. Cunnings has much to profit by Lady Sylvia," replied Gavin, "whether fortunes are good or ill at Southjoy Mission. In either case, he facilitates matters and derives a fee for both."

"Mr. Raith, you are toying with me, and I do not like it. Speak plainly. If you have news of merit, I should be glad of it."

"Then consider this," said a confident Mr. Raith. "I have learned through reputable sources—highly reputable, mind you—that there is land to be let by Southjoy Mission. What do you think of that?"

"What is there to think of it?" asked Mrs. Crandesol peevishly. "It is common enough knowledge, and I have heard the airy platitudes ascribed to that proposition."

Gavin smiled comfortably. "They are indeed airy if the true reason for the proposition is to shore up a treasury that is overtaxed by the expenses of renovation."

Mrs. Crandesol was quiet a moment and then concluded, "A most encouraging thought, Mr. Raith, most encouraging. It is a matter that will bear some watching."

"I would venture to predict," said Gavin, suggesting in his most insinuating tone that it was already a certainty, "other irregularities may soon come to light, if you do not sleep on your watch."

Regarding him slightly askance, Mrs. Crandesol acknowledged her understanding with a slight nod. Whatever agenda Mr. Raith might be pursuing for himself, he was proving to be a useful ally for hers.

"Another cup of tea, Mr. Raith?"

Chapter 20

An unusual momentary peace had settled on Southjoy Mission, a rare hiatus from the striking noises of construction and the sweeping rush of servants. Mellow of thought and mood, Lady Sylvia allowed herself to drift into an aimless meditation, aided by the golden, earthen hues of the tea that ever so gently released fragrant wisps of steam from the cup that she tenderly suspended in front of her. It was a moment to be relished with openness and candor.

Predisposed thus to unguarded thought, the flickering shadow of a pensive furrow intermittently scurried across her brow. When, after a time, a soft sigh indiscreetly escaped from Lady Sylvia's meditation, Ariana resolved to inquire as to its cause.

"Lady Sylvia," she prompted, "you seem very deep in your thoughts today."

"Forgive me, my dear," she replied, quickly recovering from her reverie. "It seems I am, though I cannot say for certain why."

"Indeed you are," asserted Isabella with a hint of amused petulance, "and you have been ever since you returned from Bath, where," she added, "you had ventured rather mysteriously for some purpose quite alone."

"From Bath?" asked Lady Sylvia. "Well, yes, I suppose that must be it," she added without further explanation.

"Will you not tell us then?" asked Isabella with feigned disappointment. "It was perhaps a gentleman that you went to see?" she teased.

"Isabella!" exclaimed Ariana. "You are too young for such impertinence." She paused, smiling, and then continued, "I, however, am not. Lady Sylvia, could it be that you met with a gentleman?"

Lady Sylvia did not respond immediately but rather considered the question with more attention than was expected.

"Whether or not he was a gentleman, I cannot say, and I suppose it is that very thought that has disturbed my peace."

"Lady Sylvia," declared Ariana apologetically, "please forgive me. I had only meant to tease. I had not meant to pry."

Sensing there might be more to this response than the address of an indelicate question, Gwyneth discreetly whispered to Carlton, "Perhaps we should withdraw to the small sitting room so Lady Sylvia may speak unreservedly with Ariana."

"No, no, my dears," said Lady Sylvia, "there is no need for that. There is nothing so indiscreet that you cannot hear of it." She took a long sip of tea as she gathered her thoughts. "It was Mr. Raith I met in Bath."

"Mr. Raith?" asked Ariana, now clearly confounded and more than a little uncomfortable. "You met him by design?"

"Yes," replied Lady Sylvia as a matter of fact. "It was prearranged, you see, to conclude a matter of business I had with him."

"Perhaps Mr. Raith was acting on behalf of Mr. Stacey?" asked Ariana.

"No," replied Lady Sylvia, "though I might have preferred it so. No." She sighed. "And now I may as well tell you the whole of it. I can see you will not rest until you have all the details."

Lady Sylvia settled further into her chair and again looked into her cup of tea where she had found so many times before a simple comfort that often could quell an unruly mind.

"I suppose it will be simplest to tell it to you as it happened," she said, whereupon she related the visit of Mr. Raith, how she had learned of his investment, and how it came about that she expressed a particular interest in such an opportunity.

"You see," she said somewhat sheepishly, "as Ariana already knows, I have spent rather a lot of money on the restoration already, rather more, in fact, than sensible moderation would have advised and as indeed you, Ariana, did advise. Should those debts fall due at the same time, I should be hard pressed to honor all of them. So you see, on hearing what could be gained, I fear I was persuaded to think, *Here is a means to redress the balance of debits and credits.*"

"But do you not risk losing a great deal more," asked Ariana, her concern as much apparent in the look upon her face as in the tone of her voice, "if the venture should fail?"

"The risk is undeniable," admitted Lady Sylvia, "but Mr. Raith seemed to be exceedingly confident, and he had, after all, risked his own fortune in the same venture."

"And have you inquired of their progress?"

"No, Mr. Raith was most particular about that. He was insistent that no undue attention be drawn to the investment because any public attention could jeopardize the entire affair. In point of fact, I have left the matter of progress in Mr. Raith's hands, and I rely upon him to convey to me any news worthy of my concern."

"And is it the lack of news that is now disquieting to you?"

"No, I was prepared to wait for developments to unfold at their own pace. No, what disturbs me and will not let me rest is the incongruity of the character of Mr. Raith and the generosity of his offer." Seeing a look of mild surprise in Ariana's eyes, she added, "I know that is a dreadful thing to say about someone, but I believe in this case it is fair and accurate."

It was not an assessment that Ariana could dispute. "It is certainly not a gesture I would ever expect of him, and I must confess I cannot imagine magnanimity as a hidden attribute of Mr. Raith."

After a thoughtful pause, Ariana asked, "Lady Sylvia, would you think it amiss if I should make inquiries, discreetly of course, regarding how such investments actually work and perhaps discovering something about investments in South Africa? I could say that as your assistant it could be valuable to know how such things work, not to suggest that I would be your advisor in such matters—that would be exceedingly presumptuous—but that I should know where and with whom to obtain such advice."

"I think that would be both sensible and tactful," answered Lady Sylvia, somewhat decisively, "and, indeed, advisable. I cannot make such inquiries myself, of course. I have promised as much. But if you were to do so on general principles, it should be harmless enough and not infringe on my promise." Then, with deeply held fondness, she commented, "How I have come to depend on you, and how dependable you have become." Though it did not fully quell her anxious humor, the observance of Ariana's evolving maturity was at least cause for some consolation.

Miss Ariana Atwood, for all her cleverness and determination, had absolutely no idea how one learned about investments or even how one discussed such matters. Certainly there was no other woman in her acquaintance who would have such knowledge. Indeed, it was a rarity for a woman to have sufficient means to be engaged in business affairs beyond what she could accomplish through her own labor. The late Lady Henrietta, Countess of Bath, of course, was a notable exception, and were that accomplished woman yet living, Lady Sylvia could reasonably have conversed with her regarding her experience in managing a vast estate, but not so at present for Miss Ariana Atwood. Consequently, her only sensible recourse was to appeal to Mr. Cunnings. He was, after all, already familiar with her responsibilities at Southjoy Mission and would not dismiss her as foolish, no matter how out of the ordinary the request might seem.

As expected, Mr. Cunnings was quite amenable to rendering a service to Lady Sylvia, which he offered without hesitation. "I believe I can be of some small service to you, Miss Atwood. In my opinion, I can say with some confidence that Lady Sylvia's own banker, Mr. Jacobson, is by far the most suitable person to consult. He is not only widely respected as a banker, but as it happens, he is also said to be very successful with his own investments."

Acting on Mr. Cunnings's recommendation, Ariana eagerly sought an interview with Mr. Jacobson. Her request, however, was nearly rejected without consideration, for Mr. Jacobson's secretary was remarkably curt and had not the least inclination to sympathy for

Miss Atwood. Upon the mention of Lady Sylvia, however, he offered to address her petition to Mr. Jacobson, cautioning as he did so that Mr. Jacobson was excessively busy at the present hour.

"I believe she is employed as an aide to Lady Sylvia at Southjoy Mission," he reported to Mr. Jacobson. "She further indicates that she has come on the recommendation of Mr. Cunnings."

"Mr. Cunnings has sent a girl to seek my advice?" Mr. Jacobson was appalled at the very thought.

"Perhaps Mr. Cunnings did so because it is a matter of interest to Lady Sylvia," suggested the secretary.

"Lady Sylvia, you say? Then you think it is not on her own account that she requests this interview?"

"I think not. I should be much surprised if she has any account at all. Certainly she has none with us."

"I see. If it is a matter of interest to Lady Sylvia, then I suppose I must make some allowance for that. I shall see her, but impress upon her that I have but the briefest of moments to spare for her—and that at a great inconvenience to me."

In the end, he did receive her, of course, out of deference to Lady Sylvia but preferred to ask more questions than he answered. In the course of the interview, such as it could be managed, when mention was made of investments in remote regions such as South Africa, Mr. Jacobson seemed visibly incensed by the suggestion.

"Miss Atwood," he said, "let me give you this one word of advice since you seem unadvisedly keen on such ideas. Many people think that the more exotic the investment is, the greater the profit is sure to be. Nothing could be more distant from the truth. Indeed, I should say the more exotic the investment, the faster the ruin. Put it out of you mind, Miss Atwood, and do not think on it again."

In the end and in a rather abrupt manner, he informed Miss Atwood that if Lady Sylvia should have any serious question regarding investments, she should address them to him directly.

The interview being thus concluded so brusquely, Ariana was momentarily taken by a sense of abandonment, like that of an orphan left stranded on a street corner with no one further to whom she could turn for aid. She consoled herself that she, at least, had the comfort of returning to Southjoy Mission and would be welcomed there. As she surrendered to the steady monotonous rhythm of the carriage, her thoughts returned again and again to the words Mr. Jacobson had spoken. Being most particular to recall every nuance of his stern manner, Ariana decided that Mr. Jacobson, in truth, had intended to chastise her only a little, just enough to leave her thoughts disturbed and troubled. Certainly his words were somewhat biting and harsh, but they could not have been more aptly pointed if he had sharpened them against the questionable wit of Mr. Raith. Indeed, Ariana found herself convinced that Mr. Jacobson, in a somewhat circuitous manner, was acknowledging her own capability, for in his own way, he was implicitly trusting her to communicate his warning to Lady Sylvia.

It was not a comforting thought, though, for if affairs in South Africa were as grave as Mr. Jacobson suggested, then Mr. Raith could not have misguided Lady Sylvia more if he had attempted to do so deliberately. It was most disconcerting, and the conclusion now looming before her caused Ariana to sigh very deeply, for she dreaded the task it entailed, that of persuading Lady Sylvia that Mr. Stacey must be informed.

Mr. Jacobson was astute in all matters of business, particularly those that involved confidentiality. In his experience, he had come to understand confidentiality as a commodity of value in and of itself. The retention of a confidence could tip the balance of a negotiation in the favor of a client, while the sharing of a confidence at a strategic moment could inspire a client to laud his service. His reputation was such that no one of merit ever voiced a concern for discretion, and indeed, should any mention of it be made, he might well take offense.

Miss Ariana Atwood had come to him, not as a matter of business, but as a matter of education. In that respect, there was nothing confidential in the event. It was that understanding that gave him leave to write a brief note to Mr. Cedric Stacey: "As you are the familial guardian of Lady Sylvia's affairs, by virtue of your inheritance from Sir Waverly Sylvia," he wrote in conclusion, "it has been incumbent on me to impart this information to you. While Miss Atwood is an able enough young woman, her interest in such investments is ill advised. You may rest assured that I have attempted to dissuade her from that course in the strongest of terms."

Chapter 21

Mrs. Crandesol beamed a pleasant welcome to the ladies she had invited for afternoon tea under the sponsorship of the Society of Native Architectures and Gardens. Among her guests were wives and mothers representative of all the trades people and skilled workmen who had been engaged by Lady Sylvia. No mention of the cause against Southjoy Mission, nor of Lady Sylvia, of course, had been noted in the invitation that brought this select group together. Rather, it was said to be a purely social occasion in recognition of the valuable service these fine workers provided to the community.

"Ladies," announced Mrs. Crandesol, "we shall begin momentarily, but first, I should be most pleased if I might say a word to all of you before we begin. We must all have our little speeches, you know." It was a small attempt at humor to which the ladies politely responded with a smattering of smiles.

"We are so pleased," she said warmly, "that all of you could join us today. As you all know so very well, the Society of Native Architectures and Gardens is dedicated to preserving the beauty of our shire. But," she now said more earnestly, "it is you, your husbands, and families who are the real heroes in our campaign. The skills that you provide make it all possible."

The smiles raised upon the ladies' faces, some self-conscious, others more assertive, reflected their appreciation of this recognition. Nodding her head to emphasize the truth of her proclamation, Mrs. Crandesol continued more humbly, "That's why we have determined that one of our roles should be to find opportunities, such as this one today, to express our appreciation for your efforts."

Looking thoughtful, she explained, "You ask not what should or should not be preserved but rather what must be done to make it so. That is why, when inviting you here today, we have held you to answer not for the task, but for the quality by which the task is performed." She allowed a hint of a smile as she added, "Even those of you who might have some small role to play in that most objectionable restoration project at Southjoy Mission are most welcome here." As the last trace of her smile faded, she concluded, "Indeed, though my opposition to that project has not diminished in the least, it is my fervent wish that none of you suffer from its failure. So let us think no more of that unpleasantness today, and let us all rather enjoy our tea and scones."

As tea was served, Mrs. Crandesol noticed with some satisfaction that a certain disquieting hum, spawned by her reference to Southjoy Mission, had entered the conversations taking place about the room. She glanced approvingly at Mrs. Droutsworthy who was responding to a question that seemed to be worrying several ladies at once.

"I do believe you are correct, my dear," said Mrs. Droutsworthy. "If I recall correctly, Lady Sylvia did suggest there was no financial difficulty obstructing her project. But then," she added with some degree of incredulity, "I find I must wonder about this letting of fields at Southjoy Mission."

"You don't think it's as they've said, then, that it's to make Southjoy Mission profitable for everyone?" someone asked.

"That may be, certainly," said Mrs. Droutsworthy, "but I must ask, who shall have the first profits of it, and what will be left for others?"

"I do not say there is a cause for this interest in profit," added Mrs. Krumsuch in support of Mrs. Droutsworthy, "but it does seem peculiar to me how rumor and fact seem to go hand in hand in this situation."

Emboldened thus to speak, the mention of Southjoy Mission could soon be heard in every conversation about the room, and to all who cared to express their concerns on this topic, Mrs. Crandesol readily extended a profusion of solicitous sympathy. Soon, cause and concern could not easily be distinguished from rumor and innuendo, and the latter two were soon accepted on equal terms with fact, for it is well known, repetition can make a robust certainty out of the slenderest of allusions.

Chapter 22

Lady Sylvia sat stiffly in Sir Waverly's study. Another communication had been received from Mr. Cunnings. The rumors of financial distress at Southjoy Mission had intensified inexplicably. It seems several of the tradesmen's wives returned home in an uncommonly agitated state following an afternoon of tea at Mrs. Crandesol's home. They confronted their husbands with such fury that the latter gentlemen had undertaken to organize a work stoppage that would take effect imminently unless reassurance refuting the rumors was forthcoming immediately from Southjoy Mission.

Now, as Ariana related the events of her expedition to Bath, Lady Sylvia was finding it difficult to resist an encroaching sense of fatigue, a need to succumb to contrary wishes, perhaps even to surrender to the reputed heritage of Southjoy Mission.

"Mr. Jacobson was most insistent," said Ariana, "and would admit of no occasion for exotic investments, as he called them."

When she hesitated, Lady Sylvia prodded, "Go on."

"No particular investment was ever addressed, you understand, but when I mentioned South Africa, he seemed almost angry with me. It was as though he knew of every detail and disapproved of the whole of it intensely. I am persuaded that his words were not intended as friendly advice but as a warning to be heeded without fail."

Ariana looked directly at Lady Sylvia as she concluded, "Lady Sylvia, I know it will pain your pride to do so, but I believe you must reveal to Mr. Stacey all that has happened. If the outcome should be dire, it would be better that he knows of the situation from you now while there is yet hope for a favorable result."

Lady Sylvia closed her eyes with resignation. Increasingly of late, it was not she but events surrounding her that determined the shape of the path she traversed in her journey from one day to the next. "I am persuaded," she said, her voice trailing into a distant whisper. After a moment, she rallied enough to say duly but without enthusiasm, "I shall make arrangements immediately. There are other matters I should attend to in London as well. I should be away no more than a fortnight." She shook her head in further confirmation of her resignation to the unpleasant task ahead.

Recalling, then, the communication from Mr. Cunnings, she looked intently at Ariana, "I shall have to impose another burden on you. We cannot afford a crisis with our creditors. I must rely on you to address the workmen in whatever manner you think necessary to ensure that their good efforts might not be tarnished." The empathy reflected in Ariana's eyes as she acknowledged Lady Sylvia's instruction eloquently expressed her understanding and her loyal, wholly dependable commitment to Lady Sylvia.

"Well, then," said Lady Sylvia firmly, "let us be off to our respective tasks."

Chapter 23

Mr. Stacey was in a dark mood as he stood peering through the window. Listening to his friend, Gavin Raith, his thoughts were already filled with expectations of affairs darker still.

"You have confirmed then," he asked with a taut firmness, "the details of Mr. Jacobson's letter?"

"That and more," answered Gavin, with the arrogance of innuendo already coloring his words. "I fear, too, your suspicions regarding Miss Atwood are undoubtedly confirmed as well."

Though Mr. Stacey clinched his fists, he remained otherwise still, saying nothing that might disturb Mr. Raith's recitation.

"It appears now that Miss Atwood's scheming has been far more extensive than you could have conceived. It is no longer just a question of letting fields to local tenants. That venture of Miss Atwood could at least be argued to have a rational benefit." He glanced downward, shaking his head as though deeply disappointed. "Now, I must report that Miss Atwood's interview with Mr. Jacobson was not mere idleness. Indeed, I must tell you, Mr. Jacobson's advice was not heeded."

Flushing with the crimson shades of anger, Cedric whirled to face his friend. There was no cautious disbelief in his countenance now, no measured restraint, only an incipient fury constricting his breathing, straining his posture, and distorting his regard until it radiated woe unto anyone who would dare to defy him in his presence.

Fueling this ire, Gavin continued in the most solemn of tones.

"Sadly, it appears Lady Sylvia has invested a substantial amount in a South African trading venture that seems certain to fail. That there should be no doubt as to its prospects, I myself researched the investment and ascertained in my own assessment that it was, indeed, highly imprudent. Were I confronted with such an investment, I should take offense at its impropriety. I do not say that Lady Sylvia is a fool, but I can imagine none but a wastrel who would accept such an investment."

He paused to stare at Cedric to emphasize the gravity of his conclusion. Seeing Cedric's anger mounting to the very precipice of eruption, Gavin brought to the fore the one aspect of his report that he believed would rivet the attention, and perhaps seal the fate, of Cedric Stacey.

"In these affairs," he said slowly, "the role of Miss Atwood has been quite prominent, so much so that her activities are keenly watched. I am told that because of her dealings, creditors have become excessively concerned about the mounting debts at Southjoy Mission, and there is now a threat of a work stoppage unless the financial soundness of Southjoy Mission can be affirmed. In short, I am afraid your tolerance of Miss Atwood is going to cost you a very substantial sum if Lady Sylvia is to escape disgrace."

Cedric whirled again and began to pace, his hand gesturing in the air as his thoughts were engulfed with the turbulence of anger, strained by the imminence of disgrace, and inflamed with unrestrained fantasies of retribution. Into this mélange of emotions, an inexplicable sense of betrayal intruded, subtly but insistently, like a latent premonition of his trust sullied and his judgment tarnished.

After a moment, he stopped pacing and stared into the distance as though he could see beyond the byways of London, past the arches of Southjoy Mission, and into the conspiratorial parlor where Miss Ariana Atwood worked her manipulations of Lady Sylvia.

"I must go there myself," he said resolutely. "I shall leave at once." Fortified by this resolution, he said briskly, "Thank you, Gavin, for your loyalty. I ask but one more favor, that you say nothing of this to anyone."

"Of that," replied Gavin, "you can rest assured. I shall say nothing. I shall acknowledge nothing."

Chapter 24

The hour was not late when Cedric arrived at Southjoy Mission. His entrance, however, was without ceremony, and he made no allowance for customary forms. Brushing past the servant who opened the door to him, he marched with firmly footed steps into the parlor where Ariana awaited him.

Ariana had spent an intense part of the morning in negotiations with the workmen. Word of Lady Sylvia's hurried and unexpected departure from Southjoy Mission spread quickly from servants to workmen and thence in rapid journey to Mrs. Crandesol, who received the news in uncommon ecstasy. She straightway called upon the tradesmen, journeymen, and their wives, exhorting the workmen to likewise abandon the premises.

"There can be no doubt now," she declared righteously. "The curse is at hand, and it has come to

Southjoy Mission. Soon, very soon, all who have dared to disturb its abode will languish in its grasp!" If there were any who hesitated or doubted her word, she had but to declare, "Lady Sylvia has fled to escape its fated grip, and there is your proof." Whether any believed the curse or not, the sudden and unexplained departure of Lady Sylvia gave credence to a curse of another sort, a financial curse they could not endure, and it was on that basis that a delegation was formed and dispatched to Southjoy Mission.

"That is nonsense," Ariana had argued when the delegation of workmen confronted her. "A curse come again to Southjoy Mission? Such foolishness. Were it true, I would have departed too on the instant. But as you see, I am here, and there is no curse."

But it was to no avail.

"Begging your pardon, miss, we mean you no disrespect," the spokesman for the workers had replied firmly. "We have our orders, and they are to beg an audience with Lady Sylvia herself. If she'll not be speaking to us, we'll not be working for her, not today anyway."

"But Lady Sylvia is away to London," suggested Ariana reasonably. "Can you not postpone your decision until she has returned? I am certain she will speak to you without delay."

"That's as may be, but we'll not risk further loss, if loss it proves to be. We bear you no ill will, Miss Atwood, nor Lady Sylvia for that matter. There is none of us who wants aught but to finish our work here, but as matters stand, we are instructed that there'll be no more work without the personal assurance of Lady Sylvia. We ask no more than that and no less."

With naught more to gain or gainsay, the workmen, honorable in their own right, departed with due respect conveyed to Ariana, who retired to the study to contemplate this rejection of her appeal. The encounter had left her fatigued and somewhat encumbered by a lethargy that threatened to consume what vitality her spirit might yet possess. She had rallied, though, refusing to be dejected, and had just begun to compose a letter to Mr. Cunnings to enlist his aid when she was alerted to Mr. Stacey's arrival.

For a moment, she could but stare at the servant. Mr. Stacey at Southjoy Mission and not in London where he ought to be? Her mind rebelled at the thought of further disequilibrium. Surely it was nothing more than fatigue that had cast her into a disturbing dream and she too far gone to weariness to will herself awake. Alas, no, there was to be no forthcoming waking, for the servant prompted again, "Will you receive him, miss?"

Surrendering then, Ariana acknowledged, "Yes, of course." Rising to her feet and disregarding the pen that dropped from her hand, she left off her letter writing and walked slowly to the parlor to await Mr. Stacey.

Cedric arrived with a brusque wave of his hand, announcing while still in stride, "I need no refreshment. I need no courtesy. I wish only to speak to Lady Sylvia at once."

Ariana, who had become familiar, if not accustomed, to the discourteous entrances of Mr. Stacey, replied sincerely, "I regret to inform you, Mr. Stacey, Lady Sylvia is away. Indeed, she has gone to London with Isabella and had expected to see you there. I fear there is only myself to attend you. But if it is some matter of Southjoy Mission that has brought you here, then perhaps I may yet be of service to you."

In the long hours of his journey, Cedric had contrived to envision Miss Ariana Atwood as an ogre, an odious shrew who schemed with merciless villainy against her superiors. But the Miss Atwood who stood now before him, regardless of her appearance of apprehension, was naught but an image of softness and vulnerability. He faltered in his resolution but then brusquely swept aside all reservation.

"No!" he suddenly chided, "No, Miss Atwood. Pretensions of innocence indeed! This will not do. This will not do!"

Ariana drew up her eyebrows in the greatest astonishment, but being dumbfounded by an undeniable ignorance as to the cause and concern of this incivility, she made no reply.

"I have come on a very grave matter, Miss Atwood, and my purpose is to determine its full degree of gravity. In truth, I require very little in the way of facts, for I am in possession of the greater part of them already. You shall supply the rest."

Ariana's bearing changed but in the slightest degree as she replied, "In that regard, Mr. Stacey, it is not a matter to be questioned. I shall, of course, endeavor to tell you whatever I can. If there is some knowledge I may offer you to aid you in your course, whatever that may be, you need but ask for it."

Cedric looked down imperiously on Miss Atwood.

"Do not think to distract me, Miss Atwood. You shall answer me here and now, and you shall not equivocate. I shall abide no prevarication of any nature."

"Of course, as I have said—"

"You have full access," he rather more accused than asked, "to the ledgers regarding the renovation of Southjoy Mission?"

"Yes, Lady Sylvia felt—"

"Southjoy Mission is at present beset with a financial crisis, as has been reported to me, is it not?"

"It is true that expenses have mounted rather faster—"

"And in spite of that situation, you have consulted Mr. Jacobson regarding investments known to be risky?"

"Not in spite of circumstances, sir, but because of them. I thought he might—"

"In South Africa?"

"Yes..." Her voice faded into a stare of uncommon perplexity as no other response seemed possible.

"And contrary to Mr. Jacobson's advice, Lady Sylvia now stands to lose a substantial sum in just that very investment?"

More than a little bewildered at the tenor of Mr. Stacey's attack, for surely that was its intent, Ariana took a moment to reply, and when she did so, her voice faltered and betrayed the anxiety that threatened to engulf her.

"I cannot deny it. Each day, it appears increasingly likely—"

"Likely? It is more than likely, Miss Atwood. It is a virtual certainty!"

Ariana took a step backward, retreating from the angry, denouncing glare Mr. Stacey now trained intently on herself.

"She trusted you, gave you privilege above your station!" he accused her, rather launching his words like projectiles aimed to inflict injury. "Have you no regard for the disgrace, the ridicule, the ruin that Lady Sylvia could suffer?"

"Mr. Stacey, I—"

"It is all as I have imagined," he declared, "and worse. It is intolerable, Miss Atwood, intolerable, and I cannot knowingly abide it. The obligations of family forbid it."

He paused only then to peer disdainfully down upon her like a condemned criminal cowering in wait of a sentence. When at length he spoke, it was in a slow, resonant execution of the syllables he addressed to her.

"Miss Atwood, I must now act in the best interest of Lady Sylvia, and I take charge of all matters on the instant. Your services are no longer required here. Please see to your personal belongings at once. I shall arrange a carriage for you, and you may depart as soon as you are ready."

With that, he turned with no further word spoken, no ceremonial tribute given, and departed the room nearly as abruptly as he had entered it.

It was some moments, though, before Ariana could move. She stood motionless in a stupor of disordered reality, frozen in the fixation of a bad dream turned to nightmare, like one unable to run from an approaching evil. She trembled perceptively as she struggled alternately, first in the throes of anger flaring in the fuel of disbelief and then in the paralysis of outrage subverted by humiliation.

Slowly, ever so slowly, her deepest resource willed her revival to a conscious, rational bearing, to a semblance, however slight, of Miss Ariana Atwood. Dazed, she walked slowly but with purpose in search of Gwyneth. Though her step faltered, though she yet trembled, no tear betrayed the ache that had seized her whole being with frightful intensity.

Chapter 25

It had been some centuries since the walls of Southjoy Mission had echoed with the tremors of tragedy, but such was the effect of the forced departure of Miss Ariana Atwood, exiled without explanation to anyone, however trusted, be they family or servant. Ariana's ashen countenance and unsteady pace had frightened Gwyneth when Ariana came to inform her, "We are to leave."

Despite Gwyneth's entreaties, seconded by a much dismayed Carlton, Ariana would offer no further account of her situation. In her slow and deliberate demeanor, however, Gwyneth sensed the imprint of injustice, the craven malice of condemnation, and, perhaps above all, the painful injury of wrongful humiliation. Questions, she understood, would have to be deferred. Together they gathered their belongings and, with Carlton's assistance, departed Southjoy Mission without ceremony, but not without the good wishes of the servants who risked censure for their demonstration of sympathy for Ariana.

In the days that followed, the affairs of the household were conducted with many furtive glances and curtly spoken words, hushed that they might not be overheard, might not be misconstrued as insolence.

Finding Ariana's unfinished letter to Mr. Cunnings regarding a work stoppage, Cedric immediately dispatched a curt but civil message to Mr. Cunnings: "I am not familiar with the details of this issue, but I am aware of the recent gossip and can, therefore, guess at its cause. Please do me the favor of announcing that all manner of work should proceed without further interruption, that I personally endorse Lady Sylvia's plans, and that all expense may be accounted to me, as may be necessary."

Creditors and work crews alike were overjoyed by this pronouncement. Servants, however, firmly and unreservedly loyal to Lady Sylvia, were not especially overjoyed by this progression of authority but understood without exception that Mr. Cedric Stacey was to be obeyed and without hesitation.

For his part, Carlton felt adrift and unsettled. Though Cedric had instructed him to continue, he knew that his effort had lost its focus and definition. For inspiration, he was drawn to look among his sketches, the early ones that had been found too dark for Ariana. How filled with light they now seemed, for in the absence of Ariana Atwood, Southjoy Mission had become a tomb, darker than anyone could recall, darker than even his earliest sketches could anticipate. The brightness of Ariana's spirit had empowered everyone to strive with diligence. Now, the absence of her vitality bore like a heavy load on the entire household.

The note he had received from Gwyneth had helped to revive his spirit. She longed to see him, and how truly he longed to see her. With the intensity of love and the faith born therein, she had appealed to him—Ariana was desolate. Was there nothing he could do?

As he looked now at the painting he had begun, *In Homage of Miss Ariana Atwood*, his fingers played with the frayed edge of the little book he held in his hands, *The True and Right History of the Heresy of Edmund Plagyts*. Carlton was probably the only living person who had read the entire book. Gwyneth had thought it might inspire him, and it had. *The True and Right History* had shown him how Southjoy Mission had persevered in the most noble of manners in spite of the abundant abuses it had to endure, much as Ariana herself must have envisioned it. But there was more to the *True and Right History* than an account of heresy and abuse. It told of the arrogance of a class of people so absorbed with their own superiority that they boasted of their own history. Its author, Carne De Sol, was one of those self-absorbed individuals who ensured that he was prominently noted in the *History*. Clearly ambitious, he was proud to be known as the Dawning Scourge because of his predilection for torturing the accused just as the promise of a new morning began to break. He declared himself a descendant of Karne de

Solis, who, one could infer from the text, was not fond of the peasants of Northumbria, as he championed the plunder of its villages and monastic settlements that were unable to defend against the armed assaults. What intrigued Carlton on reading this portion of the *History* and what now consumed his thoughts was that if Karne de Solis begat Carne De Sol, could it be that Carne De Sol begat Crandesol? If true, then the Crandesol fortune would be owing in large part to the plunder of defenseless English villages and undoubtedly to the seizure of the estate of Edmund Plagyts, for the declaration of the guilt of Edmund Plagyts was no less than a declaration of the forfeiture of all that he possessed. Southjoy Mission itself, according to the account set forth in the *History*, was looted for the sake of "cleansing the evil spirits" that might be lingering in its corridors. If Carne De Sol was as much villain as braggart, then, like Karne de Solis before him, such booty would not be left unclaimed.

It would explain a great deal, most particularly the vehemence of Mrs. Crandesol's opposition to Southjoy Mission. Should any hint of this history be revealed openly, it would ruin her standing in the community, regardless of how ancient the offense might have been, and if it were judged to be true, be it by gossip or by jury, she would be devastated, personally and socially.

But what if it were untrue? How could such damage, once inflicted, be undone? Such was Carlton's dilemma, for similarity was not proof.

Certainly it would be easier to leave the present times in its mostly comfortable ignorance of this distant past, and were it not for the devotion he prized for Gwyneth, Carlton might well have found that course preferable. Such a course, however, to be blind to a truth and deliberately so would haunt him endlessly because of the good that could come of it and because of what it would mean to Gwyneth.

Carefully considered, there was only one avenue that would achieve what his devotion and duty demanded. He must speak to Mrs. Crandesol, and he must do it unflinchingly but privately, person to person, where all could be said—or as much as might be needed.

Carlton was received coldly by Mrs. Crandesol. Her face was marked with the misshapen shadows of dark brooding. Such was the ill intent of its expression that had such a countenance marred the clouds of a broaching storm, it would have alarmed any hardened sailor who beheld it.

"Your petition was most irregular, Mr. Garrick, most irregular," she accused, "and I cannot say that I was pleased to receive it. Do not think that by allowing it I have afforded you any privilege whatsoever. You are in the employ of Lady Sylvia, and the blight she would foist upon our good English countryside does not recommend you to me in any manner. On that subject, I am adamant and shall exhibit no sympathy for you whatsoever, none at all. That is the truth, and you should know it at once."

Carlton considered this greeting soberly and then asked with genuine interest, "You are fond of the truth then, Mrs. Crandesol?"

"Certainly," she replied. So unexpected was this question that she quite forgot to express her indignation at it.

"It is the one thing that unites all artists. It is their common quest."

"How very admirable, I'm sure."

"Sometimes it is a transcending truth held in common by all humanity. Sometimes it is a hidden truth—sought by some, suppressed by others. Sometimes it is spiritual, sometimes merely factual."

"Mr. Garrick, I am certain you did not request this extraordinary interview to lecture me on artistic truths."

"Not to lecture you, no. But it is vital for you to understand that truth in all its aspects has an important bearing on art, on both its expression and its perception. Indeed, both the truth and the suppression of truth can influence how we think about art."

Mrs. Crandesol frowned. "Mr. Garrick," she declared, "if you continue thus, I shall have no further patience for you."

"For example," he continued unperturbed, "in the studies I have undertaken for my work at Southjoy Mission, I have discovered truths long hidden—whether lost, suppressed, or merely unnoticed, I cannot say. But now discovered, they have strongly influenced how I have portrayed its past history and the reformation that is underway."

At the mention of truths long hidden, Mrs. Crandesol stiffened, and her impatience changed remarkably to an uncomfortable uneasiness.

"In the end, of course, the truths about a place are intimately related to the truths about the people who have populated its history. In the case of Southjoy Mission, I have discovered a remarkable document detailing an event of inquisition that occurred at this very place. It is called *The True and Right History of the Heresy of Edmund Plagyts.*"

Mrs. Crandesol, clutching her hand to her heart, had suddenly turned very pale.

"I see you are familiar with the book," said Carlton.

"I know of no such book!" protested Mrs. Crandesol vehemently, but she was contradicted by the distress of her disobedient posture.

"But you know the story it holds," pursued Carlton with an unyielding insistence. When Mrs. Crandesol did not respond, he continued. "It is a story of an unauthorized Inquisition on English soil, of its principals as much as of its victim. It tells of men such as one Carne De Sol, who was a descendant of the much-despised Karne de Solis, and of the riches they extracted by means of the brutality that went unchecked in a savage age. As he glorifies in himself, Carne De Sol boasts that 'like the talons of the gryphon that grasp its prey in fatal grip, I grasp those who in heresy would abide.'

It is a reference, I believe, to a picture of a bird-lion creature such as might be found in a coat of arms, like the one you display there above your mantle."

"Please, Mr. Garrick," she suddenly pleaded, "say no more of it," and then added in a subdued tone so plain as to attest to its sincerity, "for clearly you know the rest."

Her breathing was now shallow and irregular, and she found herself compelled to look away from Carlton for fear of what she might perceive in his regard of her.

"Yes, Mr. Garrick, it has long been rumored in our family that there was such a book, but after such a long time, we had to assume, prayed even, that the book, if indeed it had existed at all, had perished in some abandoned tomb or grave."

Feeling a need for time to think, she asked in a tone layered with suspicion, "How did you find it?"

"I didn't. It was Miss Ariana Atwood who found it, and her sister, Miss Gwyneth, brought it to my attention because it might direct me to a course of discovery concerning the truth of Southjoy Mission."

"So you have said," said Mrs. Crandesol sourly. "Ariana Atwood, I might have known. She is a most annoying young woman, a disagreeable woman with pretensions beyond her station. I understand she has been dismissed for just such cause."

"Her cause was, and is, just, and her honor remains intact," said Carlton rather factually, without umbrage, without haste. "But we were speaking of Southjoy Mission."

Mrs. Crandesol covered her eyes with her hands briefly, then, clinging tenaciously to her dignity, even as her spirit clamored for retreat, she gathered her strength to ask, "What is it you want?"

Speaking then in softened and reasoned tones, Carlton replied, "I want most that there should be no further injuries caused by an event so long past. An injury perpetuated for some three hundred years is surely unjustified in any view of humanity."

It must have seemed a most unexpected desire, for it caused Mrs. Crandesol to lift her eyes to look at him closely, no doubt to judge the sincerity of his words.

"It is not my intention to encumber you with demands," said Carlton, "but rather to place before you a simple request." Which request, however, he prefaced sternly, saying, "I do not believe you have been honest in the position you have taken against Southjoy Mission. Indeed, I believe you have been fearful, and because of that fear, you have not been truthful. That same fear has led you to be selfish and to disregard the respect due others." He paused just long enough to observe a hint of color rise upon the cheek of Mrs. Crandesol. Then he continued less sternly, "But, I have not come to impeach the illness of your comportment nor to belabor its false demeanor. I have come to request you, to invite you, to go to Southjoy Mission, to see my paintings and drawings, to walk the grounds, to see the mansion, and to observe, wholly and without prejudice or inhibition, the true beauty of Southjoy Mission. I ask, in essence, that you see it as a labor of humanity, that you seek in it the artistic truth of all the wounds and scars that it bears, and when you have found it, and only then, judge it as you would a work of art."

Mrs. Crandesol, her mind now racing with possibilities, studied him closely and then ventured, "What you ask might come at a very great cost to me, Mr. Garrick, much greater than you might think."

"Not a cost," replied Carlton, "but an investment, one with returns so handsome they will do you honor and do it honestly."

"And if I do what you ask, you will forget what you have discovered?"

"I think I shall never forget it, no matter how I might try. Its story cries out to be heard, for it is a truth that lives on in many lives. But I am persuaded that if you accept my invitation, I shall never need to think on it again. Of that, I am certain."

Thoughtful, head bowed, her hands now folded in front of her, Mrs. Crandesol slipped into a deep mediation, far absent from Mr. Garrick. Centuries of deceit and deception were pared away, peeled away like a curtain being drawn back to let light into a darkened room. Slowly, then, she began to experience a determined and wholly inexplicable sense of relief, as though something knotted tightly about her inner conscience had been eased. Nodding almost absently in her meditation, she acquiesced to Carlton's request.

"I will do as you have asked," she said in a voice whispered from very far away.

Chapter 26

Lady Sylvia peered anxiously out the carriage window. From the moment she had received word in London, where Mr. Stacey ought to have been, that her nephew awaited her at Southjoy Mission, she had been unable to escape a pernicious palpitation running through her veins and accosting her senses like drums beating a call to arms.

As their carriage now approached Southjoy Mission, Isabella remarked, "There's Mr. Stacey, waiting."

He was standing at the entrance, his stance firm and challenging. It was a sign bad enough, but, worse, he was looking confident and patient.

Lady Sylvia had set out from London without delay or extensive preparation. Now, weary from the long journey and worn by the dismay that had disturbed her sleep for many nights, she nonetheless summoned the resources to say in her most resonant voice, "My dear Cedric, how relieved I am to find you at last. We have much to discuss."

She stepped past Cedric with neither pause nor glance and marched without hesitation into what she now fully expected to be the battleground of two determined wits.

"Please ask Miss Atwood to join us," she instructed a servant.

The servant, however, hesitated and then looked furtively to Mr. Stacey.

"She will not be joining us," Cedric informed Lady Sylvia. "She is not here."

"Not here?" asked Lady Sylvia, clearly puzzled. "Then where—?"

"I have dismissed her."

The dread that had been niggling at the corners of her mind now erupted over her like the torrid waters of an implacable flood. She stared at Cedric in disbelief, the firm grasp of incredulity denying her any possibility of response. Instead, slowly and with unsteady step, she edged backward the two paces needed to reach the nearest chair, into which she sank with a heavy descent.

Refusing nonetheless to believe that circumstances could have turned so decidedly against her, she rallied enough to gasp, "Whatever have you done?"

"My dear Lady Sylvia, that is a question I might well have asked you but for the fact that I already know the answer. As to what I have done—"

"What is it you know?" demanded Lady Sylvia. In the clearness of her conscience, she was suddenly alert and prepared to answer any conceivable accusation.

"Very well," replied Cedric, who fully expected some degree of resistance. "I shall enumerate the facts as I have them. I know that Miss Atwood has contrived to involve you in several questionable ventures. I know that she has designed schemes constructed to the advantage of herself or her associates. I know that she has consulted with Mr. Jacobson and has persuaded you, against his advice, to invest excessively in a very risky speculation almost certain to fail. I know that she has deceived you as to her motives—"

"Cedric, stop!" commanded Lady Sylvia so forcefully as to cause Cedric to look upon her with complete surprise. Standing now and squarely facing her nephew, she declared heatedly, "I cannot begin to tell you how preposterous and stupid you have been!"

Stunned by the intensity of Lady Sylvia's anger, as well as by the harshness of her indictment, Cedric winced, his eyes blinked, and his mind blanched in a paralysis of wit. So keenly was he disoriented, coherent words would not come to his lips, and were he prostrate rather than vertical, one might well surmise that he had been bludgeoned into his present silence.

"Miss Ariana Atwood has done nothing without my consent," declared Lady Sylvia, her voice still ringing with indignation, "nothing we have not discussed at great length. Her conduct in all matters has been exceedingly admirable and her loyalty unquestionable."

Having thus rectified the most horrid of Cedric's misperceptions, Lady Sylvia paused to calm herself and to ameliorate the verbal assault she had launched in anger.

"As to her interview with Mr. Jacobson," she continued factually, "it was to assess what blunder I myself may have made on the advice," she emphasized, "of your own associate, Mr. Gavin Raith."

It was now Mr. Cedric Stacey who listened in disbelief as Lady Sylvia continued. "It was Mr. Raith who arranged the entire affair and conducted the transaction."

Struggling with an irreconcilable confusion, Cedric replied harshly, more from frustration than in accusation, "Forgive me, Lady Sylvia, but that seems hardly possible. Mr. Raith assured me that he himself had researched the very investment in which you placed your funds and had determined that only a wastrel would partake of it so great was the certainty of failure."

"How odd, for he assured me that he had invested a very substantial sum of his own and, indeed, anticipated a most handsome profit in the very near future."

The disparity of these two remarks prompted both Lady Sylvia and Mr. Stacey to fall into silent reflection, for such was their mutual respect that neither doubted the other's report. After a moment, Lady Sylvia roused from her meditation and, in the most practical of manners, recommended, "Mr. Stacey, I think a cup of tea might do good service to us both. It will, perhaps, restore a proper balance and orientation to our thoughts."

Mr. Stacey, still deep in thought, acquiesced without comment.

Chapter 27

Ariana stood before the large window in the Atwoods' parlor gazing into the small grove of oak trees that bordered the side of the house.

"It will be a long winter," she said almost absently to Gwyneth. "The squirrels have given off their playing and have taken up in earnest their task of gathering nuts."

She spoke more to break the silence that surrounded her than to convey news of any merit or significance. Since her return, everyone had spoken in hushed phrases and had avoided all manner of conversation relating to gentlemen of any circumstance or of good or indifferent fortune. Left alone with naught but her own despairing thoughts, her humor had plunged into a lifeless, desolate abyss from which she now struggled to return.

As that struggle churned into the incipient flare of anger, her words came perhaps more heatedly than she had intended. "What good will it do them to work with such industry when winter will come with its snow and ice to shut them out from their treasures?"

Gwyneth remained silent long enough for the sudden ire to retreat and long enough to see the small tear that formed at the corner of Ariana's eye. Softly, then, Gwyneth asked, "Why did he do it?"

"I don't know," replied Ariana blankly, with neither anger nor dismay, nor with any surprise at the change of subject.

"Then why do you care so intensely?"

"I don't know," said Ariana with rising agitation.

"I think you do," said Gwyneth tenderly but firmly.

The silence that fell between the two sisters held but momentarily and then was softened by the deep relinquishing sigh that escaped Ariana's reserve, releasing her at last to weep.

Gwyneth rushed then to her sister, who clung to her as one clings in the throes of desperation. In such embrace may oftentimes be discovered the true grasp of reality. Even as one's spirit decries an unfathomable misfortune that has seized upon it, even as incomprehensible agony impairs the mind with inconsolable turmoil, there is yet a depth of fortitude wherein the spirit may rally, wherein a comfort may be found in the intangibles that enfold it, and if they be bound in love, it is a formidable comfort. It mattered not the cause. It mattered not the sufferance. It mattered only the need.

Chapter 28

In the soothing afterglow of tea, which was uncommonly quiet and reflective, Lady Sylvia resumed her discussion with Mr. Stacey. She calmly and patiently reviewed all that had occurred, summarizing unimportant details but paying particular attention to the exemplary role performed by Ariana. She dwelt with meticulous detail on the quandaries that befell herself and on the patiently intelligent manner in which Ariana invariably resolved them. Through it all, Cedric remained passive and still, accepting every word, every expression in attentive silence. When Lady Sylvia had concluded her dissertation, she left Cedric alone with his thoughts to make of them what he would.

Cedric sat in sober reflection, reviewing in his mind all that Lady Sylvia had said, struggling at each point to establish a commonality with what he had presumed, until now, to be the truth. But there was between the two accounts a disharmony that would admit of no concordance. Most difficult for Cedric to understand was the conduct of Gavin Raith. If the account provided by Lady Sylvia was to be reconciled with his own experience, there could be only one conclusion: Gavin Raith had been deliberate in his deceit—not of one or the other, but of both Lady Sylvia and himself. It seemed inconceivable. Repeatedly, he probed his deepest memories, but he could find nothing that would allow him to comprehend the divergent accounts.

Deep in thought, resolution of this paradox came to him, not by rational thought, but by a messenger bearing a communication from the very subject of his meditation, Mr. Gavin Raith. Cedric regarded the packet for some seconds, a certain trepidation forestalling him from opening it, for here was yet another instance not customary in the character of Gavin Raith. Counseling himself caution, he resolved to open the message, which read:

> My Dear Cedric,
>
> I do not doubt you are in some agony owing to the perplexity of your current circumstances. No doubt, too, Lady Sylvia has told you all the facts she possesses. And still you are perplexed. Your plodding, rational mind has failed you. You are in a quandary beyond your understanding. I take some pleasure in knowing that. But let us not be sentimental. You would in time come to the only conclusion possible, but leaving it thus for you to discover would deny me a pleasure that

> I have anticipated these many years. Suffice it to say, the explanation to the mystery may be found in this, that I am Gavin Raith by choice, but I was born Gavin Trayyar, son of Simon Trayyar. If that name means nothing to you, inquire of Lady Sylvia. It should be a name burned into her memory, for it was his ruin that was the making of Sir Waverly's fortune, which now is in your possession and from which I have now reclaimed a token of my own rightful inheritance, for I have no doubt that you shall indeed absorb Lady Sylvia's debt, and those that I leave behind me, received on the credit your vaunted name secured for me. If Lady Sylvia denies knowledge of this history, then you can be certain she has not the moral fortitude you claim for her! But even as I imagine it so, this she shall not deny, that vengeance has been served.
>
> G.R.

It was some moments before Cedric could rouse himself from his turbulent thoughts. One whom he had called "friend" had betrayed and abused him. Another whom he had condemned had been faithful and altogether remarkable, even admirable. In neither case had he discerned the truth.

There would be no need, of course, to be reminded of the villainy of Simon Trayyar, for Sir Waverly was very forthcoming about that history and its role in his knighthood. As for Sir Waverly's fortune, that was already well established before he was knighted, and, indeed, the distinction he achieved for the realm in that regard probably weighed heavily in his favor.

In the examination of the historical record of Sir Waverly, there surely would be found no justification for the vengeance claimed by Gavin; of that, Cedric was certain. Too often, vengeance is but a ready narcotic taken to alleviate the painful malfunction of shame. To the misfortune of all, there is no surcease of shame in such vengeance. This, perhaps, Gavin Raith might, one day, discover.

In the quietude of his meditation, the comprehension of one difficulty began to inspire clarity in other uncertainties that had also, of late, belabored Cedric's thoughts. With that clarity came a firm resolution that stirred Cedric to go in search of Lady Sylvia. He found her in the large sitting room where she was engaged in conversation with Carlton and Isabella.

"My apologies to all for this interruption," he said as he joined them, "but apologies, indeed, now fall due, and it is I who must pay them." He held aloft the letter he bore in his hand. "I have just now received a communication from Gavin Raith that pertains to both of us, Lady Sylvia, and in some respects to all of us."

The tension that had reigned throughout the day now caused Isabella and Carlton to feel somewhat uncomfortable with Cedric's greeting. Exchanging a quick glance, they prepared to withdraw, but their departure was forestalled when Cedric motioned them to stay.

As he read the letter aloud to them, there could be traced on their faces a succession of expressions in which disbelief gave way first to recrimination and then to dismay. Into the silence that followed, Lady Sylvia whispered only, "Ariana."

Cedric looked at her intently, sensing in that unadorned observation the severest of reprimands. Acknowledging it as such, he said, "Indeed, Lady Sylvia, in the person of Miss Ariana Atwood is distilled the essence of all that has transpired at Southjoy Mission. I have acted in a most hideous manner toward everyone, but most particularly toward Miss Atwood. For the consequences thereof, for the damages done either directly or indirectly, I accept the blame without reservation."

"My dear Cedric," said Lady Sylvia gently, "confession may well be cleansing to the spirit, and I rejoice in it, but not so blame. It will profit us nothing at this moment to dwell on blame."

"Perhaps, but it was my refusal to see Ariana as she was that provided the foundation for the abuse we all have now suffered. I only saw that she was of a lower class, and I did not want to believe that someone of a lower class could be of a virtue superior to my own."

"There is a saying in Spain," said Isabella shyly. "'Poverty does not destroy virtue nor wealth bestow it.'" She blushed suddenly at her boldness. "Forgive me, Mr. Stacey," she said apologetically in her turn, "I, too, sometimes forget my place."

"No," replied Cedric, "there is never a need to pardon wisdom rightly spoken. Indeed, I can wish that I had been more open to such wisdom. I was deceived, yes, but the fault that conferred that vulnerability was my own conceit. I shall take no refuge in excuses."

As he looked at Isabella, suddenly another thought presented itself.

"The infamous fiasco with Gavin and all the displeasure that was occasioned by it, was there something more to that event than has been told to me? I find it difficult to believe, now, that Ariana would have undertaken such a scheme without good cause."

"She was protecting me," said Isabella with more than a little feeling.

"From Gavin?"

"Yes, initially," said Lady Sylvia, "and then from the malicious gossip that would have been inevitable had it been generally known that Isabella was the object of Mr. Raith's attention."

"I see," remarked Cedric in an unusually subdued tone. "You once told me that she was an extraordinary person, but I wouldn't hear of it. So keenly did I want to perceive all that she did, all that had transpired without my approval, as something ghastly, and so ready was I to be persuaded that it was so that I endowed myself with the worst of opinions."

"There is enough irregularity in all of our conducts that we must all share in the accounting of it," said Lady Sylvia, if not to pardon, at least to comfort a spirit awakening to a more austere truth than it had ever acknowledged of its own volition.

Carlton coughed to clear his throat and then said somewhat sheepishly, "I fear you may need to reserve a portion of your displeasure for me as well."

As Cedric and Lady Sylvia turned toward Carlton, there could not have been drawn upon their faces a greater aspect of hapless resignation than if Fate itself, in a surly mood, had suddenly announced to them in its most menacing tone that it was not yet done with them. As all looked to Carlton for explanation, he carefully related the details of his discoveries in the *History* and of his subsequent confrontation with Mrs. Crandesol, undertaken without anyone's approval.

When he concluded his account, Cedric, increasingly contrite, said, "Then, I have misconstrued more even than I had suspected. You, Lady Sylvia," Cedric acknowledged, "suspected there was something more to Mrs. Crandesol's inflexible opposition, but I fear I gave no credit to that notion whatsoever. Now we know how infallible your instinct was."

"Not infallible," suggested Lady Sylvia. "I merely allowed for the possibility. Ariana did too, as you may recall. It was Ariana who first observed that despite the disagreeable nature of Mrs. Crandesol, there was still a good person to be found beneath her hostile exterior. In truth, there was lacking only an understanding of why her meritable goodness was not manifest in her conduct, and now, thanks to Mr. Garrick, we know even that."

Cedric fell silent and became noticeably absent from the conversation. In the passage of but a few minutes, the regimented world of Cedric Stacey had been set adrift and its order turned into a most ungainly disarray. Planet and sun held not to their proper, ordained alignment. Master and servant appeared juxtaposed. Worse, he could not escape the cacophonous echo of his own angry words that now mercilessly plunged him into a deep meditation.

As he struggled to reorder the thoughts once held so rigidly in his mind, his studious regard came to rest, solely and fixedly, on Carlton's most recent painting, but not the painting in whole, not the atrium with its warm shadows and colorful flowers. It was the assured, guileless, contemplative face of Ariana Atwood that had captured Cedric's attention and now held sway over it. She stood there beside the flowering arbor, composed and at ease. To be sure, it was a good likeness of Ariana, but for Cedric, there was something more than her physical likeness that persuaded his thoughts to linger on her image. Her face, her bearing? Skillfully rendered, certainly, but, no, the artist had infused it with something more, something beyond the image, an impression, perhaps, or an aura. As his thoughts focused, a sigh, deeply evoked from a conscience too long silent, escaped Cedric's controlled bearing. In it came realization and admission that what he perceived in the painting was a suggestion of integrity for which a mere physical description would be inadequate.

"You have captured her essence," said Cedric into the silence that had settled around him, but he heard not what may have been replied, for when a truth too long suppressed is suddenly freed, it sometimes swells to an exaltation that overwhelms all other conscious thought.

In the mind of Cedric Stacey, the charge of injustice reared like a wounded beast, straining and irrepressible, the same injustice by which he had so fervently reproached a guiltless Ariana. His inflamed conscience now demanded of him an explanation, an understanding, of how he truly could have been so callous as to take pleasure in seeing the hurt upon her face. Reproach turned to ashen despair as his thoughts leapt to a conclusion too long left wanting: a character as equable and resilient as Ariana's would not admit such hurt if it were not born of innocence and suffered in no less than love.

"You must excuse me," he said with sudden firmness. "There is yet another matter that demands resolution, and I must not let it tarry a moment longer."

Without further word and with disregard for any attempt at decorum, Cedric turned and departed.

Chapter 29

An early frost had punctuated the chill of the morning and had emoted a brilliant glint of sunlight on the fall leaves. The freshness of the crisp air was disturbed only momentarily by the reverberations and echoes of hooves beating against the hardened ground. The rider steered his horse to an abrupt stop before the house, whereupon he dismounted and announced his presence with several urgent knocks upon the door.

The arrival of Mr. Stacey at the Atwoods' home was greeted with hushed tones. Hurried and muted exchanges spread rapidly through the small household. A reluctant housekeeper, leery but subdued, ushered the visitor into Mr. Atwood's study. There, Mr. Atwood, standing squarely and solidly before Mr. Stacey, listened to the few words tersely addressed to him by Mr. Stacey. After a moment, he nodded his understanding and his approval of Mr. Stacey's request and forthwith left Mr. Stacey alone in the study to await the presence of Miss Ariana Atwood.

Ariana felt unsteady as she, in her turn, now stood before Mr. Stacey. The piercing intensity of his gaze incited nearly unbridled apprehension in her own. Yet, how desperately she longed to hear, wanted him to say that he did not scorn her existence, that she was forgiven of aught there was to forgive. Yet, how desperately she feared that he would speak at all, for if he spoke at this moment of any matter of lesser importance than the injury of her spirit, then she would know that the core of her existence was irredeemable and its flame forever quenched.

For a very long moment, an instant maybe, an eternity perhaps, silence held and bound them in a ruthless grip. Mr. Stacey would speak but for a mind that struggled against the inadequacy of his own words. He would proclaim what most earnestly filled his heart but for the recriminations that flooded his every thought. He would aspire for his words to be heard with understanding but for the abomination in which he held them himself.

Ariana swayed faintly forward. In every instant of silence came a diminution of her hope. In every word left unspoken came a condemnation of the very pretense of those same hopes. Inexorably, an unhampered strain pulled the remnants of her conscious will toward exhaustion until, suddenly, her reserve surrendered to fatigue.

"Mr. Stacey," she gamely whispered, "I fear I must sit."

As she stretched her hand weakly toward a chair, Cedric rushed forward to take her delicate hand into his, grasping it firmly and guiding her with the support of his own arms into the chair. The warmth and strength she felt in his touch inspired her senses, detaching them from her fatigue and freeing herself to look, for the first time, plainly into his eyes. In the slowest of progressions, she watched as Cedric settled into a kneeling position at her side, still holding her hand, but softly now. In that touch, confusion was chastened, dismay banished. Calmly and of a certainty, she discovered in the regard of Mr. Stacey a vision of unfathomable tranquility that was meant for her alone to see.

A smile, soft and true, gently graced her lips. "I shall be fine now," she said weakly. "Truly," she promised.

As the silence began to recede, her spirit rallied, and a quiet warmth wrapped about her words as she asked, "Would you sit, Mr. Stacey?"

His countenance returned the soft radiance of her regard, but, no, he shook his head slowly, and "No," he said to her in the most comforting of tones. "If you are to sit, then I must kneel, for the one who is adored should not be placed in lower estate than the one in whose heart you are most reverently and ardently esteemed."

Chapter 30

A hush of extraordinary proportions settled over the Atwood home. It was the sound of banished dismay, of relinquished torment, of chastened duress, and it gave way to the deep sigh of austere contentment, of merciful gladness, and the heraldry of thankfulness. Upon the succession of days and nights, there could once again be perceived the awakening of pleasantry in the discourse of both family and staff, and when thoughts were put into words, it was finally without pretense.

"You are to return, then, to Southjoy Mission?" asked Mr. Atwood.

"Yes," replied Ariana with a soft sincerity readily welcomed by her father, who was understandably cautious in his concern. "Lady Sylvia was most earnest in her invitation, and I was too in my reply. I believe I could not have it otherwise, for I have become quite passionate about it."

Seeing a shadow of worry upon his face, Ariana slipped her arm through her father's arm, accepting the comfort of his protection.

"You must not think it rash of me. I could not bear that. It is just that I feel strongly that as now goes the life of Southjoy Mission, so also goes mine. My life was suspended there when I left, and now I am to rejoin it, and I shall live again."

Ariana smiled comfortably into a light breeze that flowed softly over her face and playfully stirred through the longer tresses of her hair transforming them into gently waving banners. Beside her, Mr. Atwood peered reservedly into the horizon beyond which, he knew, stood Southjoy Mission. That knowledge had been a comfort to him in the recent past, and it would, perhaps, be again, but not so just yet. Quietly, addressing the question that was most at struggle with his thoughts, Mr. Atwood ventured, "And Mr. Stacey?"

Ariana turned to look into her father's eyes to lessen his distress by her own assurance. "Dear Father, how much you ask in your innocent questions. I assure you I am well. Cedric has returned to London for the moment. He has many matters to resolve there, thanks to Mr. Raith. But he will join us as soon as possible at Southjoy Mission for an extended stay, very extended I hope. We have much to discuss, he and I. There is much in our hearts, and it will take some time in the telling of the whole of it."

"And you harbor no regrets?"

"No, Father, none. At least none that pertain to me or to Cedric. Other people have strewn between us dense clouds of deceit and deception, but those have now dissipated, and they have vanished. In all that we have done, we have, each of us, been true to our principles and to our honest natures. More than that, we cannot ask of anyone. At Southjoy Mission, we shall now have a time, free of false impediment, to let our hearts and minds and our very souls do likewise."

Epilogue

In the darkest of moments, there may yet be light enough for hope, and in what we most dread sometimes may be found the antithesis of fear.

Mrs. Crandesol peered apprehensively down the stairs leading into the dampish cellar at Southjoy Mission. Her steps, slow and unsteady, made furtive by her reluctance to proceed, were nonetheless steadfastly propelled by a resolution not of fear, but of dignity, a dignity of such ordinary and unpretentious proportions that she had never before possessed it.

Her hand rested against the stone wall to steady her balance, and where her fingers lay, the cold of the stone impinged on her senses in vibrations as frenetic as the wail of a distant agony. Momentarily she closed her eyes, not to escape the bleakness of the cellar nor to repel the intrusions of guilt into her imagination, but to perceive and accept her own frailty and that of others. In such infirmity was to be found both cause and witness to the abuses inflicted here in the distant past and in the not-so-distant present.

When she again opened her eyes, it was to banish that fearful weakness, to rebuke the dread that once stayed her from the most just of resolutions. Firmly, she willed herself to edge forward, to extend her foot as though stepping through the recesses of time, each descending step taking her deeper into a chasm of ignominy, until, at last, she stood face-to-face with Lady Sylvia who silently awaited her at the bottom of the stairs. The two women stood wordlessly, each regarding the other, each with her own private, inexpressible thoughts.

After what seemed like a very long moment, Lady Sylvia said quietly, "We are none of us without flaws."

Mrs. Crandesol, shoulders squared, her gaze unwavering, replied firmly, "But we are free to be less so."

It was confession; it was absolution. And in its simplicity was the radiance of virtue.

In the contrition of her heart, Mrs. Crandesol felt the stirrings of resolution rallying to a fervency of action. Therein, Mrs. Crandesol could finally, and with unflinching insistence, acknowledge the wrongful suffering of Southjoy Mission. Lest there should be any doubt of her sincerity, she commissioned a monument, modest and free of ostentation, in simple homage to Southjoy Mission. Upon it, she had inscribed merely these few words:

Where thou doth cast thine eye,
Let beauty there be found
That when thou looketh with earnest glance
Upon mine humble self,
There shall a noble heart be gleaned
Amidst the whorls and gnarls
That are the garments of mine life.

Appendix

A Brief Account of the Historical Context of *Elegance and Simplicity*

The story and characters of *Elegance and Simplicity* are wholly fictional. Authentic settings, events, and people of history, however, are referenced as part of the fabric of the story. The historical context, which spans more than four centuries, enriches the story and provides it with a more credible framework than might otherwise be supposed. To allow for the enhanced pleasure that a knowledge of that particular history may confer upon the story, the following account is set forth to summarize the major components of the time line and of the historically real people, places, and events cited in the work. Any inaccuracies in this presumptuous glimpse of history are wholly the inadvertent and unintended misgivings of the author and should be forgiven as a furtherance of the fictional nature of this work.

ca. 1380: Lollardy, a religious movement that is often cited as a forerunner of Protestantism, began in the early 1380s. The movement is attributed to the writings and teachings of John Wycliffe, a theologian, biblical scholar, philosopher, and Oxford University professor. Among his many accomplishments, Wycliffe is credited with promoting and publishing the first English translation of the Bible, making the holy scriptures accessible to anyone who could read English or have it read to them. The practice of Lollardy was problematic for the Church of Rome and sometimes for the ruling classes of the countries where it was exercised. The practice thus being considered intolerable, Lollards were persecuted as heretics. One of the last of the Lollards to be persecuted, an Englishman named Thomas Harding, was condemned for heresy in 1532. The heresy trial of Edmund Plagyts, created as part of the story of *Elegance and Simplicity*, was set in the year 1503 and was patterned after the heresy trials of the Lollards.

1431: Jehanne d'Arc (Joan of Arc) was tried for heresy and sorcery by an ecclesiastical court of the Inquisition, presided over by Pierre Cauchon, Bishop of Beauvais. While England accepted neither a Papal Inquisition nor the Spanish Inquisition and did not convene an Inquisition of its own, accounts of the trial of Jehanne d'Arc indicate that it was conducted at the behest of the Duke of Bedford, Regent of France for the king of England. In *Elegance and Simplicity*, the allusion to this event was used to allow for the dark possibility of an unauthorized Inquisition at Southjoy Mission, although the *History* itself only refers to it as a trial for heresy.

1489: England and Spain negotiated the treaty of Medina del Campo, providing terms for military cooperation with respect to France, a reduction in tariffs between the two countries, and the arrangement of a marriage contract between the eldest son of Henry VII (Arthur Tudor) and the youngest daughter of Isabella I and Ferdinand II (Catherine of Aragon). The marriage, however, was delayed with further negotiations and did not occur until 1501. In *Elegance and Simplicity*, the occasion of the treaty provided the motivation for the construction of Southjoy Mission.

1600: Giordano Bruno, philosopher, priest, playwright, poet, and heretic (eretico straordinario!), was executed in Rome for heresy. As a youth, he was educated at the Monastery of Saint Domenico where he eventually became a Dominican priest. However, he soon developed a philosophy that must have been considered radical for that time period. It incorporated wide-ranging ideas, such as a notion of a heliocentric universe, the workings of memory, and an atomistic view of material objects. His writings suggested that God was in all things and in all that was natural law. His ideas so clearly offended the church that his writings were listed on the Index of Forbidden Books. As a wandering scholar, he became widely known throughout Europe, arriving eventually in England. He drew the attention of British royalty, particularly King Henry

III, and he had at least one personal audience with Queen Elizabeth I, which event was subsequently cited as evidence of his heresy. While Bruno was not mentioned explicitly in *Elegance and Simplicity*, the character, Edmund Plagyts, was loosely modeled after him.

1680: Sally Lunn arrived in Bath. Her legendary bun still delights visitors to Bath in the twenty-first century! As Ariana declared in *Elegance and Simplicity*, "nothing could be more excellent" with a cup of tea.

1771: Construction of the Assembly Rooms was completed, built by John Wood the Younger. The Upper Assembly Rooms consisted of a Ballroom, a Tearoom, and a Card Room, all of notable splendor and all linked together by the centrally located and suitably splendid Octagon Room. In *Elegance and Simplicity*, these elegant rooms provide the setting for the ball in honor of Lady Sylvia.

1774: Construction of the Pulteney Bridge was completed, built by Robert Adam for Sir William Pulteney. The bridge incorporated the highly unusual feature of shops lining both sides of the bridge. In *Elegance and Simplicity*, Mrs. Atwood and her daughters took great delight in perusing those shops.

1775: The last of the thirty houses in the Royal Crescent was completed, as designed by John Wood the Younger. The design was such that the houses were affordable by the newly affluent middle class, and some of the houses could even be let for a short period of time, usually to coincide with a particular social season. In *Elegance and Simplicity*, the proximity of the location to the Assembly Rooms would have been convenient, but as noted by Mr. Atwood, it would have been unlikely that lodgings would be available on the very short notice allowed for the ball.

1781: The Battle of Jersey was fought on January 6 between French attackers and British defenders. Jersey was a British naval stronghold of strategic importance near the French coast. The French force, commanded by Baron de Rullecourt, consisted of approximately two thousand men, only about half of whom successfully arrived on the island for the battle. Upon recovering from the surprise of the attack, the British defenders rallied under the command of Major Francis Peirson and quickly defeated the invaders. While casualties were not extensive for battles of that era, both Baron de Rullecourt and Major Peirson died from wounds suffered during the engagement. Papers seized after the battle revealed that Baron de Rullecourt had acquired plans of the fortifications, armaments, and personnel on Jersey prior to the invasion. The papers included evidence that treason had played a role in the gathering of that vital information. In *Elegance and Simplicity*, the Battle of Jersey provided the setting for the events leading to Sir Waverly's knighthood, and the related act of treason by Gavin Raith's father became the seed of Raith's vengeance aimed at Sir Waverly's wife, Lady Sylvia, and his nephew, Cedric Stacey.

1795: The new Pump Room was completed. Its construction began under the design of Thomas Baldwin and was finished by John Palmer. Patrons of the restaurant could (and still do) drink a glass of the warm water taken from the "King's Spring." Its unusual taste, "pungently piquant" said Gavin Raith in *Elegance and Simplicity*, is said to derive from its forty-three minerals with small amounts of iron, calcium, sulphates, and sodium chloride dissolved in the water. These waters were considered therapeutic already in the time of the Roman occupation, and in the seventeenth century, it became fashionable to drink the water as a curative beverage.

1795: Sydney Gardens opened, designed by Charles Harcourt Masters. "It would be very pleasant to be near the Sydney Gardens. We could go into the labyrinth every day" (Jane Austen, Letter to Cassandra, January 21, 1801). In May of 1801, Miss Austen moved with her family to a house directly across from Sydney Gardens, number 4 Sydney Place, where she lived until early 1805. Although Miss Austen was not widely acclaimed as the author of her famous works until after her death in 1817, Gwyneth may well have been thinking of Miss Austen, or people of the merit of Miss Austen, when in *Elegance and Simplicity* she wondered what "celebrated and notable people have stepped upon these same paths," said in reference to the labyrinth in Sydney Gardens.

1796: Sydney Hotel, also known as Sydney House or Sydney Tavern, opened, in the design of Charles Harcourt Masters. It served as the entrance to Sydney Gardens, which made it an elegant and fashionable place for entertainment. It was especially renowned for its galas. Not originally designed with sleeping quarters for guests, the hotel was modified in 1836 to accept lodgers. A public announcement of the time (The Holburne Museum Collection, item number 1992.4: Publicity card) entitled, ROYAL SYDNEY GARDENS, AND PULTENEY HOTEL, BATH, read, in part,

> H. Seymour has the Honour respectfully to announce to the Nobility, Gentry, and the Public, that the above Establishment is now open for their reception. – The extensive additions and improvements made to the hotel enable H.S. to offer such accommodations that he trusts will conduce to the comfort of those Families who may Honour him with their Patronage, and whose continued support it will be his constant endeavour to deserve.

The building is now the home of the Holburne Museum of Art. In *Elegance and Simplicity*, a small literary license was invoked to allow lodging at the hotel at a somewhat earlier date, ca. 1808.

1803: Henrietta Laura Pulteney (1766-1808) became Countess of Bath. She had inherited the vast Pulteney estate from her mother in 1782 and managed the estate along with her father. Among her notable accomplishments was the development of Bathwick on the east side of Bath. Additionally, she endowed two schools, one in Northamptonshire and the other in Berkshire. She became Baroness Bath in 1792 and was subsequently elevated to Countess of Bath in 1803. In *Ele-*

gance and Simplicity, she is cited as an exception to the rule of that era, being a woman of independent means and eminent ability. The painting, Henrietta Laura Pulteney (ca. 1777) by Angelica Kauffmann, found in the collection of the Holburne Museum, inspired the gowns that Ariana and Gwyneth wore at the ball held in the Upper Assembly Rooms in honor of Lady Sylvia.

ca. 1810: Ivory trading in South Africa had been pursued for many decades by the English, Dutch, Portuguese, French, and Austrians, with varying degrees of success, much of it focused on the area of Delagoa Bay. Throughout many decades in the 1700s and 1800s, it also appears that much of South Africa was the scene of numerous armed conflicts and civil wars. Between 1799 and 1803, for example, people of the Khoisan and AmaXhosa mounted an uprising against settler expansion in the vicinity of the Cape, and in 1811, the AmaXhosa once again engaged the colonists. In *Elegance and Simplicity*, these events form the basis for the infamous investment perpetrated through Gavin Raith. It may be inferred from its context that the investment may well have been intended as an illicit trading in ivory to fund a tribal uprising.

2008: The Jane Austen Festival, an annual event of the Jane Austen Centre, Bath, United Kingdom, was attended by the author and his wife, Carolyn, and special friends, Virginia and Jack. In *Elegance and Simplicity*, an idealized version of the costume assembled by the author for the Promenade provided the outfit that Cedric Stacey was wearing when Ariana and Gwyneth first encountered him at Sydney Hotel, and the special coach hired by the Atwoods for the ball in honor of Lady Sylvia recreates the author's experience with his wife and friends in hiring a carriage for the ball that was held in the Upper Assembly Rooms as part of the Jane Austen Festival.

R. G. Munro, Williamsburg, Virginia